WHEN PARALLEL LINES MEET

WHEN PARALLEL LINES MEET

MIKE RESNICK

WITH
LEZLI ROBYN
& LARRY HODGES

THE STELLAR GUILD SERIES
TEAM-UPS WITH BESTSELLING AUTHORS

MIKE RESNICK
SERIES EDITOR

an imprint of

Rockville, Maryland

Series edited by Mike Resnick.

ISBN: 978-1-61242-307-4

www.PhoenixPick.com
Great Science Fiction & Fantasy

Published by Phoenix Pick
an imprint of Arc Manor
P. O. Box 10339
Rockville, MD 20849-0339
www.ArcManor.com

CONTENTS

INTRODUCTION TO
WHEN PARALLEL
LINES MEET

G reetings, and welcome to another Stellar Guild book, the tenth in our series.

The purpose of the Stellar Guild is to team a top science fiction writer up with a protégé of his/her own choosing. The established pro writes a novella, the protégé writes a novella or a long novelette, a sequel or prequel set in the same universe, and shares a book that's guaranteed to get him or her better exposure than 98% of first novels do.

The established pros who have been featured in prior Stellar Guild books include Kevin J. Anderson, Mercedes Lackey, Robert Silverberg, Nancy Kress, Eric Flint, Harry Turtledove, Larry Niven, and Jody Lynn Nye.

For *When Parallel Lines Meet*, I invited Lezli Robyn to join me. She and I had collaborated on seven short stories, including a couple of award winners, that were recently collected by Arc Manor/Phoenix Pick as *Soulmates*. We came up with the plot, characters, and setting—and when we were done, we liked what we had but realized that we were a bit short for a Stellar Guild book. So I contacted Larry Hodges, who had sold me half a dozen stories without a reject in my capacity as editor of *Galaxy's Edge* magazine. I showed him what we had, invited him to join us, and suggested that he write a prequel to our almost-novel. These are two newcomers, Lezli and Larry, that I think you're going to hear a lot about in the years to come.

And, as always, all thanks to publisher Shahid Mahmud for okaying the Stellar Guild concept in the first place.

—Mike Resnick

WHEN PARALLEL LINES MEET

BOOK ONE

FRACTURED DREAMS

LEZLI ROBYN

ONE

When I first saw the alien, I confess I reacted from a place of prejudice, as unbecoming as that was for the Lead Interrogator in the Neuropsych subdivision of the Cartheeli Military Caste.

It was not that I had never seen an alien before. Of course I have. Indeed, I was trained to show no bias. But no one had prepared me for the repulsion I would experience at seeing its—no, *his*—form.

The fact that I could not repress that instinctive repugnance was unacceptable. I performed mind scans on other sentient species on an almost weekly basis, and some of the races I have met were the most peculiar beings imaginable. But different was not repulsive. Different was not even necessarily ugly.

Disfigurement was.

Belonging to a race that strives for physical perfection— often resulting in artificial augmentation at an early age and clone-transference at the first sign of any permanent imper- fection—I was no stranger to the vanity of our race, and to my own built-in prejudices. But I would have thought that the nature of my job would have made me more tolerant.

The alien was suspended in a zero-gravity Medicapsule, floating unconscious as three different types of bio-scanners whizzed over, under, and around his body, compiling a three- dimensional image of all his internal and external injuries to project them onto various diagnostic stations around the room. I watched one of the analytic B.U.G.'s—a Blood Utility Gauge—phase through the force field sphere surrounding the patient with quarantined air, its diaphanous wings twitching ever so slightly as it settled on his neck to take a blood sample for medical and genetic analysis.

The cybernetic bug was a perfect specimen of biotechnology—always clinically obedient, yet able to adapt to a new patient's biology with an instinctiveness innate to the biological half of its form. I did not have the time to marvel over one of the latest advancements in our medical technology, however. My focus remained unswervingly on the alien.

I advanced toward the patient with purpose, and with more than a little trepidation. This was the first specimen of this species we had encountered, and the first thing he had done was react with violence.

It is no wonder his medical condition was so precarious. We had understandably responded in kind—purely as a defensive measure, of course.

His appearance did not improve with proximity. His eyes were lidded, but I could see that they were small—hardly practical, and certainly not omnidirectional. He had not seen us advance upon him until we were almost close enough to touch him.

His skin also appeared to be leaking in physical distress, with beads of liquid forming along his brow and across his torso. I had known of other species who had exhibited that trait, so that detail was not as unusual as his skin color, which was a brown-tinged shade of the palest pink I had ever seen.

It looked smooth—soft to the touch—but there was no way I would touch any part of him. Just the mere thought of tactile contact was extremely off-putting.

I studied his overall structure and determined that his cranial circumference was smaller than I would expect for the size of his frame—a sign of lesser intelligence, perhaps?—but his mouth was eerily similar to ours. I had to admit it fascinated me that there could be any similarity at all between our races, even if his lips looked more…engorged, somehow. The hands on his upper appendages were remarkably similar, too, even if they were short a digit....

Which bought my attention back to his deformity: yet another thing he was missing.

One of his lower appendages had been completely blown off during the First Encounter, torn flesh being delicately woven back together over the remnant by a cluster of biotech spiders (which were too new to have a pithy acronym assigned to them yet). I would not be surprised if the Research Caste was using this alien to test out their latest advances—I admit to being equally fascinated and repulsed by the intricate web the spiders were weaving to bind his injury together—but even their delicate work could not detract from the disfigurement.

I looked down at my lower appendages, as if to reassure myself that my three legs were still all accounted for. Still green. Still entire. Still functional.

Most members of my race would not abide such a mutilation as that which the alien now sported, opting to transfer their brains into cloned bodies earlier than their appointed time—unless they had yet to lay eggs with their mate. The purity and sanctity of our genetic code was governed by the strictest of rules. When it was discovered that the most basic of cell structures in the clones would eventually break down without a daily cocktail of medications, a law was passed to prohibit procreation by cloned mated pairs. We could not risk the anomaly being passed on to a second generation.

Yet there were barely enough egg clutches produced to provide a sustainable birth rate, so because of that first law, a second law was passed to require the remaining mated pairs to have offspring *before* they were allowed to apply for a designer body. A greatly diminished birth pool was the price we paid for longevity—for the pursuit of physical perfection.

The alien muttered something incomprehensible, thrashing around in response to something I could not see. I moved closer to his cranium, which was curiously covered with a brown pelt, and closed all three protective lenses over my eyes to shut out all sources of light.

I sent mental feelers out, seeking access to his mind.

I could feel him mentally flinch, instinctively try to throw up mental barriers, but he was in no condition to fight. His mind was just as fractured as his body.

I slipped in as gently as I could, sliding past the Thinking and Impulse levels, too disciplined to be distracted by the—

I was hit with an onslaught of images and sounds, and was stunned by the strength of their impact.

At first they were all jumbled, all incomplete. I wrapped his mind in mine, trying to absorb the psychic flare; intent on giving him at least the impression of control again, so he could order his thoughts, and I could glean more from them.

Instead, I was stuck watching the First Encounter echo in his head, the memory becoming a nightmare as he replayed it over and over again.

I felt a moment of disorientation until I realized I was watching the scene from his point of view; from his limited visual capacity. One second he was bottling a specimen and labeling it on his inventory list, and the next second he was surrounded by "strange green Martians," the likes of which "appeared in every Roswell movie he had ever seen."

Except that these aliens were holding glowing weapons.

I was still trying to decipher the references when I realized that he had recognized the weapons for what they were, and was pulling out his own. I watched in horror as he aimed his pistol at my comrades—my friends.

They fired.

I feel a flare of psychic pain, and heard the gun go off before the scene started again. And again.

I tried to push in deeper, to see if I could reach down past his nightmare, to his inherent motivations; to discover who he was and what his purpose might be.

I had to find out if he had simply reacted out of fear, resulting in the death of—

He must have felt my intrusion, and like other aliens in the past I expected him to "push" back and instinctively throw up some kind of mental shield.

But that is not what he did. Instead he somehow locked onto my psychic link and dragged me *into* his nightmare, and this time I was the one standing in the center of the soldiers who had approached him, weapons drawn for protection....

Except that I had no weapon of my own, and he was aiming directly at me.

I felt the bullet shatter my connection with his mind. The psychic whiplash was excruciating.

It was a long time before I could open my eyes. Even longer before I could concentrate on my surroundings.

There was no doubt this alien was unlike anything I had ever encountered before.

There was no doubt he was dangerous.

I left the room, and soon after Prisoner #17537 was officially added into the Station's records.

TWO

The prisoner's eyes did not look any more impressive when they were open, and the glint in them appeared fierce.

I tried to put the memory of our previous encounter out of my mind, tried to ignore the lingering sense of unease his keen gaze awoke in me, and approached the medibed with a firm stride, wondering what it meant to see his brows furrow, his nose wrinkle up, and his lips press tight together as he watched me approach.

Was it shock? Apprehension? I presumed he would not remember his nightmare—or my unwilling presence in it—but I would have to be guided by his first words.

"What manner of creature are you?" he demanded, the biotech enhancer implanted in his neck translating his words into Cartheeli Basic.

"My name is—"

"I don't give a damn what your name is. I want to know *what* you are, and why the hell you think you have the right to restrain me." His eyes narrowed even further, if that was possible. "My people will come for me. I'm—"

"Ah! So we *are* going to introduce ourselves," I interrupted, as befitting my status as Lead Interrogator. "I am Keelarah the Soul Diviner, of the Cartheeli Military Caste, Lead Interrogator of the Neuropsych Unit." I performed the ceremony of welcome, which involved some gestures that did not translate well into words, yet generated a significant raising of his eyebrows.

Knowing his guard was down, I finished off by gingerly "pushing" an impression of peaceful cooperation into his mind.

His eyes widened, the fire diming in them slightly. "I—I am Chip…no, I mean, I am Chief Surveyor Forrest Brown…."

For a second I thought I heard "…*NOT at your service*" echo in his mind following his introduction, but when I pressed further, his eyes narrowed and it felt as if he threw up an impenetrable mental wall that seemed to belie his fragile medical condition.

I pushed again, to no avail, and this time I even detected some kind of pushback.

I retreated, more than a little surprised. I expected him to throw up instinctive barriers—most races have self-preservation wired into their genetic make-up—but he was reacting as if he *felt* my intrusion on a conscious level. Not only that, but he responded in kind. That had never happened before.

How could this alien have such strong barriers and telepathic instincts, and yet appear to be untrained? I had been educated to recognize the unconscious mental reflexes of many varied species, but it was not an impervious skill, given that I did not—as yet—know much about this alien's physiology. Could he have known what I was doing? If so, that could make my job so much harder. It was imperative I determine the threat this species posed to us.

I believe I hid my uncharacteristic uncertainty well. "What star system does your race call home?" I asked with no perceivable preamble.

"So you can go do *this* to my people, too?" he exclaimed, gesturing wildly at his leg. Or rather, at the empty space on the bed where his leg should have been.

I knew I had to choose my next words carefully. "I regret that such an unfortunate incid—"

"Unfortunate, my ass! You butchered my leg!"

"And you killed my pod-sister's mate," I replied, with equal weight to my words, if not theatrics.

An expression I was yet to recognize contorted his face. "It was aiming a weapon at me," he replied, his tone suddenly quieter and more measured. "They *all* were. It was kill or be killed."

What an odd and brutal expression, especially since trying to kill her people when he was so outnumbered would usually have gotten him killed more quickly, not less—if they had not have shown mercy. It appeared he came from an unusually aggressive species, despite their limited physical stature, or perhaps *because* of it.

I thought I would try another tactic—empathy—and get to the important questions in a roundabout manner. "We regret that we did not have enough expertise concerning your physiology to replicate your defective limb within the regeneration window, but I hope that your stay with us has been otherwise very...recuperative."

He blinked. "You...*regret?*" he responded, and somehow the pitch of his voice changed; became sharper in some way. "So you green freaks *regret* blasting my leg to smithereens?" A diagnostic B.U.G. flew through the force field to take another blood sample, but he swatted it away. "And while you're at it, keep these blasted things away from me."

"Blood sampling from that particular piece of biotech is what originally saved your life, when we nearly performed the wrong procedure on your...compromised form." I tilted my head, curious. "Does your race not have any diagnostic aides, such as these?"

"Not *living* ones. Not like these disgusting critters." He looked down at the spiderwebbing on his leg stub and shuddered. There was no other word for what his body did.

It was clear that he was an unusually combative alien. I had to try yet another avenue of information gathering. By offering up facts he must already know about our star system, it would appear that I was willing to share with him, and maybe he would offer up something about his own star system in return. "We live on the second, third and fourth planet in the Oridineese Star Coalition—two of which house domed atmospheres," I informed him, knowing that evidence of our once-sprawling civilization was clearly visible on all those planets, but neglecting to mention the extensive Cartheeli Military Installation beneath the surface of the outer, fifth boundary planet, in which he now resided. "Of course, I do not expect you to know much about us," I added in an overly-understanding tone, making sure to add in a hint of condescension.

"You might be surprised at what we know about you, which is why you should seriously consider it wise to let me go."

I tilted my head to the side, as if confused. Or maybe curious.

He took the bait.

"You are in what we classify as the 55 Cancri star system… forty-one light-years from…" he trailed off, eyes widening.

"From home?" I supplied helpfully, using all my training not to show my triumph.

I very tentatively reached toward his mind again—just to skim what I could off the surface layer. I was rewarded with glimpsing the image he automatically "sees" when he thinks of home: a vast domed city on a gray rocky surface, with a majestic blue-and-green planet hanging in the background.

I could not "see" enough to know what the planet was made of—those colors could be indicative of so many different minerals or gasses—but I knew that others were listening in, that they would already be determining what star systems could be forty-one light-years from here—once they were able to determine the exact measure of a light-year.

We could translate the concept, but not the exact mathematical measurements; we had never measured travel in that manner. So I "sent" my pod-brother—and fellow member of Cartheeli Military Caste—the image I had procured. It might help them narrow it down.

"You're making an assumption," he finally replied, after collecting himself. "Not all distances are calculated with home as an origin base."

Very true, but he could not know that I had seen the image in his mind; that it was mentally tagged as "home."

"Do you miss it?" I asked.

"Do I miss *what*?" he almost spat out.

"Home," I prodded.

Unbidden, an image tagged "family" appeared in the surface layers of his mind. I saw two older specimens of similar skin color, and a younger one identified as "sister" that sported a more curiously pinkish shade.

"What's it to you?" he exclaimed. "Why do you care?"

"Would you not be curious as to the origins of a guest, should one turn up uninvited to your planet?" I countered.

He did not answer, but he was clearly considering what I had said, his mental shield lowering slightly at the reasonableness of my words.

I reached a little further into his mind, and he did not react. *This is more promising*, I thought, sliding in deeper. Maybe the nightmare had simply given him an unexpected burst of mental cognizance to my presence. Perhaps all I had to do was—

Ghastly images from the First Encounter flared anew in his mind, as if prompted by my thought. I felt my pod-brother try to "reach" for me, to pull me out—but I was thrown back into a turmoil of violent images of the preceding day, and quickly lost my psychic equilibrium.

The alien's emotions overwhelmed me, and I instinctively latched onto his mind to stop my mental spiral.

"Stop messing with my brain!" he suddenly exclaimed.

I froze, my mental fingers still hanging onto the lowered shield, not sure whether attempting to withdraw would call more attention to my actions and prove him right.

Yes, withdraw! he projected. *You are shouting loud enough in my head as it is*, he added, then firmly—and somewhat brutally—tore my mental grip loose and threw my presence out of his mind.

I did not resist.

I was shocked. My psychic pathways were almost vibrating in pain.

No one, no matter what their species, should be able to *hear* my thoughts during my inspection of their neural pathways. Perhaps a prisoner would feel some pressure, or a compulsion to do something they would not normally do—such as tell the truth when I ask my interrogation questions—but my effect on its mind should be subliminal, at most; not an interactive telepathic process on the conscious level.

How was it possible that our neural pathways were compatible enough for us to communicate on such a...*familiar* level? I had thought my psychic walls were impenetrable.

I remembered that he did this during his nightmare again, and blanched a pale lime green. If he could demonstrate such control over a mind meld *while asleep*, I had no idea how powerful he could become with proper training.

I focused back on the prisoner to see his eyes were fixed on me, blazing, his fingers rubbing the skin over his frontal lobe in a circular motion. I suspected he was in pain.

Good. So was I.

I had thought he had looked vulnerable, lying in that med-ibed, so badly damaged. Yet if he could display such innate power, such callousness when so physically vulnerable, what did that tell me about the danger his species would pose to our planet—our very star system—if they were ever in a position of dominance?

I had more questions than answers to analyze after this first official session, but I was determined to find out what he had to gain by surveying our planet in a cloaked vessel that had *almost* escaped our detection.

I had been tasked with ascertaining if there was an imminent threat to report to the Cartheeli Council. I now knew my answer.

THREE

I ensured that the alien was in a malleable psychotropic stupor before I entered the military medical facility again. I would say it was for the patient's well-being, but I would be lying.

I was hesitant. For the first time in an interrogation environment, I *knew* I did not have the upper hand.

So I had decided to create it. Artificially.

I dismissed all medical staff—the patient was well monitored by all the biomonitors in the lab that the Military Caste could procure, anyway—and approached the Medicapsule. I had ordered for the prisoner to be taken off the medibed, so the alien was, again, suspended within his zero-gravity force field. I did not want him to feel any anchor to the real world when I started to work with him. I needed him to be completely pliable to my thoughts.

His eyes were open, but they were glazed, the pupils barely registering my presence when I stopped directly in front of him.

This time I did not introduce myself. I did not want him to feel any real sense of time or place. I just slipped into his mind, past the wilting shields he had no ability to hold firm.

At first I just stayed on the Impulse level, trying see what, if anything, he was instinctively reacting to in his current state. It was not anything I was not aware of. There was an overall sense of fear, a certainty that he had to stay alert, but was struggling to remember why. He retained enough rationality to know that he was somewhere alien to him, somewhere that he considered dangerous, so I deliberately did not focus on that thought. I did not want to increase his awareness.

I slid deeper, and felt a token resistance. I was in the Recall level, gently sifting through his memories for something—*any*thing—I could use.

It helped that he was actively trying to work out how he should react to this situation. Close to the surface of his memories were his training drills. He had been accessing them to try to work out the best way to respond to his current predicament.

I siphoned the memories into our collective consciousness (by "our" I meant the fellow members of my Neuropsych team, who were patched into my link for added support) and we formulated a plan.

I triggered a training scenario in his mind, based on piecing together a collection of memories. What better way to see what this species could be capable of than to see how they are trained to respond in First Encounter situations? Since he would consider it a practice round, I reasoned that he would be more forthcoming with his answers, not experiencing the edge of fear that could cause him to measure his answers more carefully.

I inserted an impression of myself in his mind with the guise of one of his dark brown-skinned trainers (how is it that this species had so many variables in appearance?) and began to mock interrogate him. Except, of course, the questions were real.

Feeling somewhat discombobulated to be "walking" around on only two legs, wearing the face of one of his superiors, and yet pretending to be the alien I really am, I leaned over the table while pushing questions in his mind.

Why did you come to our planet in a space vessel that was able to mirror its surroundings so sufficiently that it was invisible to physical sight and most military scanners?

I "felt" him collect himself and prepare his response. *By the nature of my mission, I travel alone, which would render me more vulnerable to predatory extraterrestrials, should they be able to see that I would be without aid if any calamity befell me.*

It was a perfectly reasonable answer, even if I could tell it was somewhat of a lie. They were utilizing subterfuge for secrecy purposes, too. That I could "sense."

I immediately honed in on one word he had used: extraterrestrials. I knew through our connection that it was another word for aliens; that the *extra* part implied *other*, which further implied *different*—but what did Terrestrials mean?

Was this species known as Terrestrials?

Can you explain the meaning of the word "extraterrestrials," please? I asked, with a suitable amount of curiosity and ignorance.

It basically means "Other than Terran," he replied.

Excited, I pressed on. *So you are Terrans, then?* I asked.

His faced screwed up in that strange manner of his. *No, I suppose that we would be considered…Earthlings.*

I interrupted the mock interrogation to talk to him in the guise of his trainer. *You realize that if I was an alien, you just gave me valuable information.*

His eyes widened, and I could tell his guard was down. *How so?*

You are labeling our people to the alien species.

Calling ourselves Earthlings gives nothing away about us. It's not even what we identify as.

I could not help but be intrigued by that last statement. *By saying you are Earthlings,* I continued, *you are implying you are 'from Earth', which infers that our race comes from a specific planet.*

Oh, shit, he answered, slapping his hand on the table in what appeared to be a sign of aggression. *And it also implies a specific type of planet, too. One with dirt on it. Shit shit shit!*

I fought hard to not let my eagerness show. *Yes, exactly. Aliens could use that information to narrow down search parameters.* Which was exactly what we were going to do.

So I should just say we are humans, then, he reasoned. *So it looks like I'm being cooperative, but it doesn't really tell anyone anything specific about our origins—our scope—as a race.*

So they were called humans. He was right. That did not tell me anything. I pressed on:

Your earlier answer...about your vessel, I reminded him. *Your response could be construed as acceptable, but it does not explain why you are on a planet to which you are not native and to which you do not belong, taking samples. Did you assume another species would just believe you would go to all the effort of concealing yourself and traveling forty-one light-years across the galaxy just out of mere curiosity?*

We are testing the minerals on other planets, he answered, drolly, *to ascertain if the environs are suitable for the various emerging sentient races on Earth, because they need a planet of their own, or there will be surely civil war on ours.... If I told that to another species, wouldn't they perceive it as a colonization threat?*

I was taken back. *How many species on your planet are sentient?* I asked, not sure whether to be more alarmed, or curious.

He screwed up his face again, eyes narrowing. *Are we back in training mode again? Because you are acting like you don't know the answer....* He shook his head, eyes blinking.

I did not answer quickly enough. I felt a sudden, albeit weak, "push" against my mind, and it was enough to disrupt the dream sequence.

I knew he was so heavily medicated that it would be almost impossible for him to wake up, and presumably he would not remember the encounter—but I withdrew to the surface level of his mind and opened my eyes to check his physical condition.

He was moving haphazardly around in the Medicapsule, clearly resisting something—but what?

Then I realized: he was fighting the drugs within his system.

I looked up at his face to see his eyes were blinking, pupils starting to react.

He would certainly not become more agreeable if it were discovered I had been playing with his mind again. I did the only thing I could think of: I uttered the command to turn the force field surrounding his body opaque, and backed away from the Medicapsule.

Perhaps the darkness would lull him into a deeper state of unconsciousness.

I could not have been more mistaken.

I heard strange sounds coming from inside the capsule, and could see the force field reshaping and crackling as it bulged out.

I retreated completely from his mind and glanced over at the hologram depicting his vital systems. The alien was moving erratically, his heartbeat increasing in speed.

Was he having an adverse reaction to the drug?

I looked at the levels in his blood. I might not have the expertise to understand the numbers, but I knew by their color level that they were all within safe parameters. What was wrong with him?

With the current concoction in his blood, it was too dangerous to order further sedation, but if he continued in this manner, the force field could overload and fail.

I was briefly aware that medical personnel were racing back into the room, being triggered by some kind of Medicapsule alarm. I closed all three lid layers over my eyes and steadied myself before his capsule, cautiously touching his surface mind again with mine. I had to see what was motivating this madness.

I slid no deeper than the Impulse level, and felt pain, fear... such intense fear.

Why?

I could "see" he was instinctively trying to raise his inner shields, but in his current condition was unable to. I needed to go deeper, to move from the Impulse to the Instinct level, and see what was driving this terror. My mind "closed in" around his to try to help calm his thought patterns—steady him—but the only response I elicited was a measurable increase in his fear.

It overwhelmed my senses—I simply could not think straight. All I felt was the intense need to get out, to break free of the walls that were closing in on me.

Smothering me.

Suddenly the realization dawned: he was claustrophobic!

I tried to act in the physical world, but I was all but paralyzed by his fear. The alien had latched onto my mind, and we were sinking fast.

I desperately reached out a mental tendril for my pod-brother, managed to show him what was happening in a quick burst of thought, and he immediately ordered the force field to become transparent again.

But it was not enough. The patient could not "see" the change in his mind. He was experiencing what his jumbled thoughts labeled a panic attack. He still believed he was enclosed in a small tight place.

I needed to act, to distract him from his fears, but I was stuck within the panic loop of his mind. I realized I *had* to let him know I was here for him to kick me out, for him to latch onto an awareness of the outside world again.

I "sent" him an image of a clear force field with the impression of fresh air and open space. *I am here.*

It appeared he was too fractured to reply directly, but I suddenly saw an image of an alien child who had been space-launched in a suffocatingly-small escape pod, as he watched in horror as his family's mining station exploded.

Was that you? I asked.

I felt an affirmative response swirling through the chaotic threads of his fear and despair.

It was no wonder he was petrified of enclosed spaces. I had the impression he had been stuck in the capsule a long time before it was discovered that he was still alive. The sole surviving member of his mining community.

I did the only thing I could think of. I countered his image with one of my own.

I shared images of my family, who were used to the small enclosed spaces of their pods. I could sense that my pod-brother was trying to tell me to disengage, trying to advise caution, but I ignored him and overwhelmed the alien with images of very small green infants curled up together, three to each glowing egg pod.

It worked. The alien was surprised by my images, distracted enough from his fear to find a small anchor in the here and now.

It took some time and coaxing, but eventually he calmed down, let go of my mind—gently, I might add—and came back to full awareness.

I heard my pod-brother's voice, relieved but hesitant. "Keelarah?"

I opened my eyes to find that I was looking directly into the alien's, who was now wide awake and calm. He held my gaze for a long moment, then glanced sideways to look down at his hand.

At *our* hands.

While still on opposite sides of the force field, they were clasped together, the field crackling at the contact, molding to the negative space between our hands.

I pulled mine back as if stung. Not out of fear or disgust, but from the sheer surprise at the sense of comfort that strange gesture had given me.

His gaze remained intently on me.

I turned to my pod-brother, who looked even more surprised than me. "I am well," I replied, but of course I was not. "The patient had an adverse reaction to the procedure," I added, which was very true, if slightly misleading.

I turned and walked toward the wall, before my pod-brother could sense the true reason for my elevated emotions, and paused to watch the glowing blue-green biostrand structure unweave to provide an opening, a welcome exit from the trauma I had just experienced.

I strode briskly out, raising buffering shields around my mind in the first stage of self-care. I needed to analyze what had just happened.

I was certain I had to move him to a secure cell. I had never encountered anyone of any species that could enter my mind without my consent, which gave him the potential to subvert my interrogations as he willed. Granted, I could tell in this instance it had not been a deliberate—even, conscious—effort on his part, but if he could do that to me, the Lead Interrogator, what could he do to the other members of my pod, should he direct his attention to them?

I could hear the medical personnel order some tests in the soothing click-clack tones of our language as I walked away from the room. I could feel his gaze still burning into the back of me.

I shuddered. *What have I done?* I asked myself, wondering if I was too compromised to continue on with the interrogation.

Thank you, was the answering, very human, reply.

FOUR

I awoke abruptly in my pod, feeling distinctly disoriented.
I again had to shake the errant feeling that I was enclosed in too small a space and suffocating because of it, as I had done for the past three cycles since I had last interrogated the prisoner.

Usually my pod was a source of comfort, cocooning and rejuvenating me during my sleep periods, while keeping me connected to my pod-siblings through an intricate network of organic wiring. But an echo of the alien's severe claustrophobic psychosis had somehow transferred into to my subconscious.

Each day since the interrogation I had awakened with that instinctive urge to break free of the pod's warm embrace, but today the impulse felt even stronger somehow. More intense.

Perhaps you should see a Psych Healer, my brother suggested, his advice gently caressing my mind. I felt him stir in his pod, on the other side of the Neuropsych command quarters.

My apologies for waking you up, Reymeen, I replied, feeling guilty.

It could not have been helped. This prisoner is...alarming.

I could not disagree.

I suggest having someone accompany you on your next session, if only to distract him from being able to focus the full breadth of his abilities on you.

Or you could just let the murderer die, came the distant reply of our pod-sister, Eleenari.

I was stunned. Not because of the starkness of her words—although they were shocking—but that she had responded at all. Eleenari had been placed in a form of medical coma following the death of her mate, under the supervision of Psych Healers whose specialty it was to work with the surviving partners of soul-pairings, to help them rewire their brains to such an extent that they would have a chance to survive the loss of their mate with their mind and spirit intact, if not whole.

She should not have been able to communicate with us at all.

I mentally searched for her location, to find she was still in the Medilab—but *not* in her stasis pod.

A sense of unease filled me, a feeling echoed back to me by Reymeen. I triggered the release valve in my sleep pod and waited impatiently as it started to open.

The disquiet increased in my mind. The feeling of suffocation that usually dissipated with the last vestiges of my dream returned multifold. I grabbed onto the pod opening, forcing it to open quicker, until I could clamber out of it.

I could not breathe.

I mentally called out to Eleenari, but she did not answer. I could feel she was in the prisoner's room, that despite the psychic loss debilitating her synapses—which still held onto the ghostly echo of her mate's presence—she was experiencing a sense of triumph.

I reached out to Reymeen to feel that he, too, was forcing his pod open, his thoughts torn between which sister needed help more.

Not me, I told him firmly. *Check the prisoner.* I knew he was closer to the Medilab than I was.

I reached back and touched the pod once more, using its integrated systems to send out a mental blast to the medical and security personal needed to track down my sister. Then I fell to the ground.

I reached for the prisoner, something I should not be able to do at this distance, and discovered I was already connected peripherally to his thoughts.

He latched onto my mind, his fear so debilitating it literally took the last of my breath away. For it was *his* Medicapsule that had been compromised. *He* was the one who couldn't breathe. I was just experiencing a psychic echo of his physical distress.

I felt my brother arrive at the Medilab, and sensed his frustration when he could not enter. The room's lockdown procedures had activated as soon as the prisoner's force field had been compromised. I was the one with the security clearance level needed to override the settings.

Reymeen showed me what he could see through the wall's porthole. My sister had managed to get out of the room in time, but not before she had injected the prisoner with some kind of pathogen.

What was it doing to him? I could "feel" his airways were closing; somehow swelling.

He had enough energy to send me one image burst.

You need to go to the evidence room, I told my brother, urgently. *Go get his spacesuit.*

It took a minute for Reymeen to follow my reasoning, but when he did I could feel his speed as he raced into the adjacent wing of the station.

I concentrated on my breathing, on reminding myself that it was not *my* system that was compromised, and got up. I *needed* to get to that lab.

I felt my pod-sister get tranquilized, and medical personnel surrounded her. My heart was heavy with the pain she was experiencing. Her distant presence in my mind dissipated as she fell unconscious, and I concentrated on the crisis at hand.

I made my way Medilab, aware that my quarters were a lot further away from it than my brother's had been. By the time I arrived it took all of my effort just to tune out enough of the prisoner's distress to be able to function. With shaking digits I pressed my hand into the holo interface so it could read my identity, and then entered the secondary code to authorize the override.

Reymeen arrived just as the security features deactivated and the wall parted to allow access. We approached the Medi-capsule to find the alien flailing weakly, his eyes desperately seeking mine, before rolling back into his head.

We deactivated his restraints, dragging him to the floor.

Reymeen shook out the suit, at a loss as to what to do next. *How do we operate this suit of yours?*

No reply, just a weakening of the presence in my mind.

I slapped him on the chest, and felt a faint echo of pain. *You need to focus. You need to tell me how to save your life.*

I felt him rally at my words. He managed to dredge up a memory of when he instructed his sister on how to suit up for her first moon walk.

I shared the information with Reymeen, and we got to work, my pod-brother pressing various buttons on the arm panel—activating the suit so that it opened up—while I lifted the patient.

My chest constricted tightly. I could feel the human draw in his last breath, yet his psychic presence remained, a stubborn whisper in my mind.

I lowered him into the open cavity of the suit, and the suit automatically enclosed around the alien, its monitors activating, immediately triggering some form of emergency procedure.

We watched as the suit scanned the prisoner's biosigns, a sharp device extending from one of the pipes within the base of the helmet to inject some kind of liquid into his neck, directly into his circulatory system.

He did not draw a single breath.

I sought the dying presence in my mind, unable to believe that someone with such innate power could be so weak in the end, could give up so easily.

I felt a flare of defiance and latched onto it, fanning it until that spark of life flared brighter. The oppressive weight in my chest lifted as the alien finally drew in one haggard breath and then another.

My pod-brother finished checking over the suit and, satisfied, slumped back on the floor.

I sent Reymeen a loving caress, and a thank you, and allowed the strange psychic connection with the alien to take more of a foothold in my mind, knowing it was the only thing connecting him to the here and now.

He was too valuable an asset to lose.

My last hazy thought, as we both slipped into the unconsciousness of restorative sleep, was to note that his skin had indeed been soft, after all.

And not in the least unpleasant.

FIVE

When I woke up in the Medilab, I was feeling oppressed, confused, and very alone.

I presumed I was experiencing residual feelings from melding my mind with the prisoner to save his life—that all I had to do was reach out to my pod-brother or the rest of my work pod, and the impression of isolation would dissipate—but it was helpful for me to analyze the emotions the alien had been feeling at the time we last met.

No—correction. What he was *still* feeling.

I tilted my head to the side, and "listened."

This was not a psychic memory of our *last* encounter I was experiencing, which would have had a significant amount of pain and fear dominating the emotional bandwidth, but rather I was feeling what he was *currently* emoting.

I was stunned. I had thought the only reason I had felt his fear yesterday was because he had somehow reached out to me in his distress. I had believed I could not experience what he was feeling without making a conscious effort to reach into his mind. Without him making a conscious effort to connect to mine.

There must be something about his alien physiology, or maybe his current emotional state, that meant he projected when he was not paying attention to his mental shields. I could tell that he was not aware of my intrusion; he believed himself to be alone in his thoughts.

I "reached" for my pod-sister, keen to reassure myself that she was safe before I went to work, but her presence was too weak in my mind for comfort. I consulted the Station A.I. about her current condition—she had been placed into a deeper recovery coma, with a senior Psych Healer assigned to her case—and requested a data blast of her current medical stats to go over them later.

While I knew she wasn't conscious of my presence, I sent her a soothing mental caress, then asked the Station A.I. about the current location of the prisoner, and was surprised to discover he had been moved to one of the interrogation cell blocks. I felt a pang of...was it concern? Surely, after yesterday's encounter, and with his extensive injuries, he was considered too medically compromised to move....

Until I realized that if he had already been in an interrogation room, Eleenari would not have been able to get past the inbuilt security measures to reach him.

I sought medical clearance from the nurse-bot to discharge myself, and made my way to the interrogation block all the way on the other side of the base. I could not help but be impressed by the alien's ability to "project" across such a vast distance. Or perhaps I was simply displaying my talents as a receiver of renown in my race.

I had always been able to hear my pod-siblings, no matter where they were on the base, but that was a known ability in our race, to varying degrees, especially when there was a genetic predisposition to such a connection. I should not have the same affinity with a prisoner...and an alien one, at that. Maybe his kind were simply easy to "hear."

I approached the Neuropsych wing of the interrogation block, and when I had gone through all the physical security measures I mentally sent the current password to the central control room's bio-interface, which had been programmed to accept telepathic codes only from members of the unit under my command, and various high-ranking military officials.

By now I could tell the prisoner was aware of my presence, even if he had yet to sight me. I approached his cell with a little trepidation, and oddly enough, a sense of self-consciousness.

When I laid eyes on him again it surprised me to see that he was standing, albeit with the aid of a gravity neutralizer that essentially enabled him to float until he was able to be fitted with a substitute biosynthetic limb.

Our gazes locked, and the intensity I could see in his small eyes was impressive. I tried to recover a semblance of clinical detachment and control over my emotions, but I was the first to look away, disconcerted. My gaze lowered to the empty pant leg again, which was floating distractingly above the gravity neutralizer and I was surprised to realize that I no longer felt repulsion when I sighted his disfigurement, but something else.

Pity?

No. I knew that losing one's leg was a small price to pay for killing another sentient being. He needed that lesson. I was feeling something different. Something that was not befitting a Lead Interrogator of the Neuropsych Unit.

Sympathy, my pod-brother suggested, adding his thoughts to mine.

Yes, I replied, *you might be right.* The events of the previous day solidified in my mind, toughening my resolve. I had to admit I was starting to admire this…human.

With an apologetic nudge, I pushed Reymeen out of my mental pathways and approached the force field surrounding the alien's cell. I could not seem to tear my gaze away from his leg. Or the lack thereof.

"Take a picture," he said, eventually. "It will last longer."

I looked up, startled. I could not quite get the inference of his comment, but I "felt" the reproving tone. "We are not accustomed to disfigurement," I responded, truthfully.

"And the crazy one from last night?" When I did not answer immediately, he continued. "She seemed unaccustomed to me *living*."

"She is not crazy," I replied, a little defensively. "She is simply maddened by grief. You killed her mate."

"So it's an eye-for-an-eye, is it?"

I blinked. "No, your eyes are of no particular interest to her, except for the simple fact that yours can still see, while her mate's are now closed to this life."

He considered me for a long moment. "It's an expression. It wasn't meant to be taken literally."

"Well, Nareemal's death is not only literal, but incomplete." I felt his confusion, and continued on. "It is the reason for her psychosis. In a way he is still with her...*inside* her. When two members of our race enter a soul-pairing, their mental pathways become joined."

"Soul-pairing? Like a symbiotic relationship?"

I paused, considering his words. "Yes, I suppose it is in a way, except each maintains autonomous control of their individual bodies. It means they can keep a sense of self as physical individuals, but yet be able to share each other's minds and experiences as if they were one."

The human's face screwed up in that unusual human way of his. "So did I kill him? Or only his physical form?"

"Yes," I answered, much to his confusion. "The complexities of soul-pairings go deeper than our scientific ability to properly analyze the phenomenon, but we can do scans that detect the connection, once it has been made, and those scans also show leftover...residue? No, that is the wrong word."

I hesitated, then overtly initiated a two-way connection between our minds. I sent the prisoner a series of concepts I could not quite put words to, an overall image of what I was trying to encapsulate.

He drew in a deep breath, using the gravity neutralizer to move closer to the force field—closer to me. "Ah! We call that the spirit." He paused, considering his next words. "The part of the body that is not corporeal, but gives us our sentience."

"Yes, *exactly*!" I tilted my head to the side, and was fascinated to see that he followed suit. "Without Nareemal's physical form to anchor his perception of self, his...spirit...will eventually blend with hers—warp hers—if it does not drive her mad in the meantime. He would be there, in her mind, but not."

His head bobbed up and down, seemingly thoughtfully. "Yes, we have a condition among our people called schizophrenia. It is where a person hears voices that are not real. It can be quite debilitating."

I inclined my head. "The difference here is that the leftover parts of him *are* real, but are becoming *less*, somehow...."

I stumbled again for some translatable words, sending another series of concepts to the prisoner.

"Ah!" he replied. "We would say he is becoming less human, somehow—or even, *less humane*—because he has lost the framework for his humanity."

He must have felt my confusion; it was his turn to hesitate. He acknowledged the open pathway between our minds by gently pushing an impression of what he meant into mine, so that his words could translate into an equivalent for my species.

I blinked, fascinated. "Yes! He is already a fragment of the entity he once was, losing his self-control when he lost his body, so his impulses and volatile emotions linger down familiar psychic pathways to bleed into Eleenari's, causing her to react without her usual rationality and compassion. She will lose herself in him, unless his essence is successfully extracted from her neural pathways."

"So it was Na-reem-al"—he stumbled verbally over the name, despite the biotech enhancer doing most of the translation work for him—"who came after me last night?"

I was impressed by his perceptiveness. "Yes, for the most part. Eleenari's grief probably would have always led her to your room to confront you, but it was the fractured, angry spirit of Nareemal that overwhelmed her natural restraints, that convinced her to inject you with the substance that triggered such an unusual suffocating reaction."

"We call it anaphylactic shock. Your windpipe can swell shut due to an adverse allergic reaction to a chemical, food, or even perhaps a plant nearby." He looked at the bioluminescent walls, fascinated, as if to illustrate an example.

"We do not have a…windpipe."

"I was using a plural, nonspecific form of 'you'." He studied me for a long while. Then: "You saved my life."

I met his gaze, once again. "Yes."

"Even though I killed your sister's mate?"

I answered in the affirmative.

"Why?" he asked, his gaze sharp.

I tilted my head to the side again. "One does not have to preclude the other."

His mouth flapped open, then closed again. "But you must hate me," he said, finally.

I should not have been surprised by his conclusion, but I was. "No," I said. *Hate is not an emotion easily nurtured within a race that communicates primarily by thought*, I "sent" rather than spoke. *It would be hard to contain such an emotion to oneself, since we live in such close…proximity.* I raised my hand and used one tapered digit to tap the side of my head for emphasis, then spoke out loud again: "It is my resolve to ascertain the purpose of your visit—of your species—through professional investigation. Nothing more." Except my conversation with this unusual alien felt everything but professional.

I felt him reach deeper into my mind, presumably to ascertain the truthfulness of my words.

That he could do that at all, with my standard mental shields in place, astounded me. The dawning realization that it was because I had subconsciously allowed him access *through my shields* shocked me even more.

Maybe I *was* losing my objectivity as Lead Interrogator. It just appeared that this particular alien responded better to frankness, rather than any of the more duplicitous interrogation techniques that had worked so well on other species.

"You catch more flies with honey than vinegar," he responded, as if I had spoken out loud, and I felt his agreement—approval?—of my assessment.

I did not comprehend the phrase, but before I could finish formulating that thought, the alien had solicitously pushed the explanation into my mind.

He considered me for a long moment, and I could "feel" he was on the precipice of an important decision. "We may have started off on the wrong foot," he suggested wryly, gesturing toward the absence of his leg.

I could not help it—I laughed. From his shocked expression it must have sounded unlike any vocalization his race normally produced.

"You are definitely correct in that assumption," he replied, pulling his mouth into a position that exposed his teeth. He stepped forward, even closer to the force field, and extended his hand. "I am Chief Surveyor Forrest Brown, of the Galaxy Class Ship *Wanderer*. Archeologist, botanist, explorer. Species: human. Gender: male."

I considered his hand, not immediately certain how I should respond. I recalibrated the force field to allow my biomatter to pass through it, and extended my six-digit appendage through the barrier to clasp his five-fingered one in the tactile manner of his race. "I am Keelarah the Soul Diviner, Lead Interrogator in the Neuropsych subdivision of the Military Caste; Highest Order Mindreader. Species, Cartheeli." I paused, then added privately: *Our sexual designation is not considered an important designation, except in cases of procreation.*

Is it rude to ask you what…designation, you are? he inquired via mindspeech, following my example.

It can be, I replied. *It is more that it is irrelevant. We mate on the basis of neurological rapport, rather than physiological compatibility, and vocations are not gender specific. Since we only have one soul-pairing in our lifetime, we have no need—like other races I have interrogated—to preen to the opposite sex in order to gain a mate. It means our sexual designation is only relevant at times of copulation…which is considered a very private, very intimate affair.*

The human's grip tightened, his emotions reflecting amazement as he sifted through my unvoiced surface thoughts. *You are female.*

I inclined my head. *You sound surprised.*

No offense, but you have no…uh, discernable attributes to separate you out from the opposite sex.

Remembering the anatomical analysis of his sexual organs in my report, I decided to elaborate. *I am female in our sense of the word, not yours.*

He looked intrigued.

Unlike your species, it is the male gender of our race that carry—and then bud—the resulting offspring.

I sensed his confusion. *But then wouldn't that make you—?*

No, I interjected. *I am still the equivalent of a female of your race in all ways but one.* I "searched" his surface mind for words he would understand. *If our species procreated in the same fashion as yours, I would now provide the egg to my male partner's sperm. The difference is he would be the one to "give birth" to our children, to use a Human expression.*

I could feel his interest. *How do you know when—*

There was a loud whoosh sound, I heard people enter the room, and then felt a distinct impression of fear!/panic!/danger!

I started too whirl around to confront the intrusion, but the human pulled me through the force field, flinging me behind him, his grip fierce on my hand.

I started to fight the human before realizing the turbulent emotions were not only emanating from him, but from the Cartheeli soldiers now standing on the other side of the newly-recharged barrier.

I tried to unclasp my hand, but he was unmovable. *Why do you restrain me?* I asked him. I peered over his soldier to see my comrade's gazes—and their weapons—trained on my prisoner.

"Let her go!" they asserted, almost in unison.

I began to struggle again. I had thought the human was open to discourse, to cooperating in my investigation, yet I could feel the fear and defiance I would expect him to exhibit in an attempted escape. Did he grab me to be his hostage? His leverage?

I reached deeper into his mind to direct a mental attack, only to be overwhelmed by yet another of his feelings. Something just as powerful, but distinctly different.

I stopped struggling, amazed. I was "feeling" protectiveness. In his panic, his first instinctive reaction had been to shield me.

Weapons down! I projected to the assault team. *In his alien way the prisoner is trying to protect me.*

I felt their begrudging acknowledgement and tried to mentally reach the human, to let him know that I was safe.

He did not answer. I peered back over his shoulder to see his gaze was fixed on their weapons, and then surged deeper into his mind to see his attention was focused on a nightmare that showed identical weapons shattering his leg…again and again and again.

I realized the sight of the glowing bioguns was triggering his reaction. I repeated my order, with all the authority of my position. *Put your weapons down.*

I could sense their hesitation. One by one the weapons deactivated, their energy source winking out as each of them powered down.

We are safe, I told the human gently, soothingly.

He blinked as if coming out of a dream; his grip on my hand lessoned, and then he let go.

SIX

When I entered the cell the next day, the human immediately glided in my direction. I held up my hand up to stall him, to ensure that he kept his distance and ascertain the force field was standing firm between us.

"We don't want a repeat of the misunderstanding we had yesterday," I told him, and a little of the intensity left his face.

"Indeed," he replied, collecting himself. "I wanted to apologize for any harm I caused you. That had not been my intention."

"There is nothing to apologize for," I informed him. "I was the one in the wrong. I can see how, at first glance on the monitors, it would look like you had taken advantage of me, especially since we must have appeared to have been fused together at the barrier."

"No," he replied, hesitating. "I meant for what happened… *after* they entered the room."

I blinked, surprised, cocking my head to the side. "You were re-living what had happened to your leg?" I prompted.

"Yes," he replied. "As soon as they came I just couldn't take my eyes of those damned weapons." He paused…then added, quietly. "I think I have PTSD—post-traumatic stress disorder. Initially from what happened to me as a child, and perhaps triggered anew by my years in service, and, well…." He gestured to the offending lack of a lower appendage.

"Yet you seemed to have been…altered by the lights on the guns," I pointed out.

"I did?" he asked, surprised. "I don't rightly remember what happened. All I knew is that one second we were talking, then I felt extreme fear, and the next moment you were on my side of the force field, *behind me*."

"Do you remember why?" I asked.

"Why what?"

"Why I was behind you," I prompted, again.

His face screwed up as he tried to recall. "Not really. I'm not even sure when they came into the room." He frowned, looking down at his hand, and it was as if mine tingled in re-membered pain. "I recall we had been re-introducing ourselves to each other…"

"Yes," I said.

"…and then the soldiers came into the room and you were vulnerable, with your back turned to them."

"They were my own people," I reminded him.

His face screwed up even more. "Yes, I suppose so…but they had guns. You did not."

"True."

"So that means I…." He looked up at me again. *I was pro-tecting you!* he projected, willingly sharing his thoughts with me for the first time since the incident.

I was surprised at how much I had missed his mental presence. *Yes*, I replied. *Now you can see why there is no need to apologize.*

He seemed about to protest, when the wall behind me sep-arated, admitting several high-ranking officers.

Ye gods! Not again, he replied, and I felt him retreat—yet not completely disappear—from my mind.

I whirled to see Adjunct Commander Travernii walk in with Reymeen and several official-looking officials.

"It had been our understanding that you would not conduct another interrogation of the prisoner without another mem-ber of your team in attendance to support you," he announced upon entry.

I looked over at my pod-brother, who had the grace to express his guilt. *We had discussed this, Keelarah. He is not safe. Or rather,* you *are not safe around him.*

I did not have the time to ask him what he meant by that last distinction. *We will talk about that later,* I told him, because I was not liking how those very official-looking officials were looking at my human.

Like they could pour gravy over me, and just lap me up, came the droll response from the other side of the force field.

I suppressed my amusement (*You know I'm right,* he added) and I walked over to the group, effectively blocking him from their view.

"How do you propose to assist me today?" I asked in the most authoritative voice a Lead Interrogator could assemble.

"We have a holoform requesting the transfer of Prisoner #17537," the first official announced.

"Who requests it?"

"The Teslarnii Research Facility—transfer purpose and doctor's name suppressed for security purposes," answered the second official.

I don't like the sound of that, the human interjected.

Neither did I. I accepted the proffered holodevice, activating it.

What is the meaning of this? I asked Reymeen on our private line as I started reading the form. *I am finally beginning to build a rapport here....*

Are you sure you are the one controlling the direction of your interrogations, or is it him? I know of at least two times that the prisoner has caused you harm....

And there were mitigating circumstances each time, I interjected. *I'm finally starting to get into his head. I think, under his layers of bravado, is someone who has suffered an intense trauma, resulting in a psychotic break. Instead of letting it destroy him, he was somehow able to build a new life around the cracks in his psyche, bolstering them, so they did not get worse. Perhaps, if I hone in on what first broke him, I can find out more about his how people....*

"You realize the request for transfer is purely routine," the second official pointed out, interrupting my stream of consciousness.

I did not immediately answer. I continued studying the holoform.

Do you think you could still hear me, if they take me beyond the reach of your moons?

I turned around to look at the human, surprised. *I think so*, I replied. *But my reach has never been tested beyond the fourth planet, and only with pod-siblings.* Furthermore, the Research Facility fell under the Intelligence Caste's jurisdiction. I suspected if I signed him over, I would not get him back.

At least, not likely in one piece.

I turned back around to look at the Adjunct Commander. "With whom can I appeal this request?"

"Lead Interrogator, you are coming perilously close to trying my patience," the Travernii pointed out. "The prisoner is not worth risking your position."

I gathered myself to protest.

"I consent to the transfer," the human announced, much to my surprise. *I've already gotten you into enough trouble, Greenie.*

I blinked, surprised to feel the warmth that accompanied those words—the inherent protectiveness.

I signed the holoform, no longer sure of anything.

SEVEN

I tried to go about my business, but Lead Interrogators do not do well without a prisoner to interrogate.

I filed all the reports I could lay my hands on to help to dispel my impression of inadequacy, and I combed all the plants in my office as they sang to me, their glowing fronds swaying back and forth as I harmonized with them.

I was feeling an inordinate need for the comfort they usually provided after a tough interrogation session, but nothing worked today. The sense of unease that had filled me since Chief Surveyor Forrest Brown's transfer ship had left planetside simply increased.

I considered the alien in question, wondering when I had stopped labeling him a prisoner in my mind. Maybe Reymeen was right; he had gotten to me somehow.

But I also knew that I affected him, too. Why else would that confounded human agree to be transferred to a Research Facility, just to save my green hide?

I sensed that what I was experiencing was a healthy dose of guilt. While I knew I had helped him through his nightmares in the past—after triggering them in the first place using scrupulous interrogation techniques—*he* had actively protected me against perceived harm twice, while *I* could not even prevent a transfer.

Simply put, in my confusion over his reaction I had given in to signing the holoform against my better judgment, and now I had more questions than answers.

I reached out across the expanse to see if I could still feel the human's presence, and the sense of relief was profound when our minds connected…until I realized the connection was so weak I would have to yell simply to even be heard.

I resisted the urge to call out to him—telling myself I had no obligation to him from this point on—and went to see my pod-sister to distract myself. She had finally been brought out of her biochemically-induced coma, and I could see the extended rest had calmed her…marginally.

Her Psych Healer had assured me they were extracting the leftover traces of her soul-pairing's spirit, and that she had been showing remarkable recovery, but it appeared all my visit did was reawaken her sense of loss.

"Did he ever show remorse for his actions, Keelarah? How close was he to death when you had reached the broken capsule? Obviously I was not in my right mind when I tried to kill him, but that did not mean you had to go to such measures to save him, either. What possessed you?"

The questions were endless, and what answers I could give to her did not satisfy—especially for the last question.

Because the answer was that I had no idea what had possessed me. Or why the alien's presence could infuriate and soothe me in equal measure, even when he was such a distant speck in my mind.

I made my excuses and left the Psych Sector of the Medilab, making my way back to my pod-room. It was well into the Base's sleep cycle by the time I returned, and I checked in on Reymeen, only to discover that his thought-patterns already reflected a deep sleep state.

I envied the sense of calm that emanated from him. I hopped into my pod, and waited for it to close around me, connecting me into its web of nutrient-filled circuits and biopathways, to help sooth my body for another day.

I knew I should have fallen asleep straight away, but I could not resist using the pod's connectivity interface to help amplify my 'reach'.

I could still feel the alien's presence, but it was dimming, almost out of range, and I could not resist the compulsion to know how he was faring.

Are you out there? I asked, hoped, yelled.

There was no answer at first, but then I felt an echo of surprise, reflecting back along the communication channel.

I am here, he finally responded.

Where is here? I asked, genuinely curious, only to be suddenly overwhelmed by an intense impression of fear, the psychic backlash of an explosion, and the feeling I was suffocating again.

I thrashed around, looking for a way out of the darkness—for a release from the relentless space that was now pressing in around my escape capsule, crushing me.

Not again, I heard him say. *Please, not again.*

I was dimly aware that my pod-brother had been alerted to my distress, that he was instructing me to breathe in and out, slowly, as I struggled for my every breath. Then he severed my communication with the human, and I felt no more.

EIGHT

I woke up to discover that I was still in my pod-room, cursing the day I ever met that confounded human, yet profoundly worried about his fate, all the same.

You're no walk in the park either, I'll have you know, darlin' came the obstinate, almost-affectionate reply.

I pulled myself into a sitting position and glanced around my spacious apartment. He had sounded so close.

Alas, I do not have such a luxurious abode as you. I'm in one of your recovery ships, about to dock at your base again.

They returned you here? I asked, incredulous.

I stood up, ignoring the holonote Reymeen had left for me, and made my way to the Emergency Services dock.

Apparently the escape pods were programmed to return their victims to your base, and they were scooped up as they were passing the nearside of your fourth planet.

I heard the quaver in his voice and reached for the memory, feeling him flinch as I replayed the explosion, noting the ejection of only a handful of escape pods. *I am sorry you had to go through that experience again*, I told him quietly, remembering an earlier image of him as a child, space-launched in a suffocating-small escape pod as he watched his family's mining station explode.

It was no wonder he was claustrophobic.

I reached the ship just as it was disembarking and waited for the alien to be escorted out of the ship's food cellar, the only room on the ship which had a lock on it that could confine a prisoner.

He was soon shepherded down the ramp by two Medilab guards, hopping between them on his lone leg (his gravity neutralizer having been left behind in the ship-that-was-no-more).

With all the commotion, he had not noticed me standing nearby, and I did not see fit to inform him, content to watch him as he slowly made his way across the hanger.

I could not help but notice he was a rather striking figure, even in his current vulnerable state. Taller than the tallest of my kind, I could tell he tried to balance his weight in such a way as to assist his bearers.

I know you are there, he said quietly. *Or rather...here.*

I stepped out into an open area and he alerted his guards to my presence.

"I did not expect to see you again," I told him, truthfully, as they approached.

He looked at me, and bared his teeth. "But I am such a captive audience."

I laughed, startling the guards more than him. The human was incorrigible. "Return him to his previous cell."

"I rest my case," he muttered, the humor dissipating.

I followed them, not sure what I should say. On one hand I felt relief that he was alive, and some kind of warmth in response to his attempt at humor. But he was still my prisoner—*my* captive. I need to practice professional detachment.

We entered into the Neuropsych wing of the interrogation block, Reymeen running out of the Communications Office to intercept me in the hall.

I instructed the guards to continue to his cell and focused my attention on my pod-brother.

"It was those humans," he exclaimed, looking excited but projecting fear.

"*What* was the humans?"

"The explosion." In a burst of data and images Reymeen projected the intel he had received from the survivor's escape pods; intel their occupants were not even aware of, it had happened so quickly.

I focused on the holocaptures of the alien ship, comparing them to the latest intelligence report on the smaller ship that had belonged to the prisoner. There was a remarkable similarity in features and design.

"They killed our people without any provocation," he added. "What if more are coming?"

I "felt" the prisoner reach for me, sensing my emotional turmoil, and threw up a shield.

"Has this footage been verified yet?" I asked Reymeen.

"No, but—"

"I expect a preliminary report as soon as it can be procured," I interrupted, rediscovering my professional detachment.

I dismissed him and went straight into to the interrogation cell. "Did you know this would happen?" I demanded, as I entered the room and approached the force field. "Did you 'send' your people a message, to come after the ship?"

"Why in universe would I want that?" he exclaimed.

"To escape," I accused. "Do not try to convince me that is not what you want."

"Of course, I want to escape, dammit," he confirmed. "But. I. Did. Not. Want. To. Die."

"You did not die. *My* people died—again." *Because of you.*

His eyes widened. "You are missing my point. Why would they blow up the ship if they knew I was in it?"

I will admit, that did give me pause. "What is it your people say: 'To kill or be killed'."

"Well, yes, that is one saying, but I do not understand how that is applicable…." His eyebrows raised in alarm. "My people are *not* murderers. They would only fire if they had just cause."

Then why does your mind express shame, I demanded, and forced my way through his shields to uncover the reason for that emotion.

At first he fought me, tried to stop me from seeing. Then he tried to explain it away. *We were young then. Ignorant.*

Your species has orchestrated mass killings! I exclaimed.

Yes, he admitted, reluctantly. *Out of prejudice, ignorance and pride…. But we have emerged from that volatile stage of our evolution. We've changed for the better.*

I reached deeper into his mind, and he let me. *You persecuted your own people!*

Yes, he agreed. *There was a time, many times, where one of our races would commit atrocities against another, simply because they could not accept the differences between the color of their skin, for one absurd example. "Them ugly green freaks are the devil's spawn. God's creatures were not created to have three legs, but two. They should be exterminated,"* he intoned.

That is what you think of us—of me? I demanded, incredulous to realize I cared about the answer.

No, dammit. He slammed a clenched fist into his thigh, hard, in frustration and I gasped. *I am saying everything wrong. I was trying to provide an example you could relate to.*

But I was no longer paying attention to his words. I was in shock.

At first I thought it was because I had never seen someone self-harm before. It was such an ugly concept to my people; just the sight of him hurting himself was appalling. But then I realized there was a more shocking, unbelievable reason for my reaction.

I was in physical pain, now, too.

I looked down at the burning, throbbing patch on my leg and then raised my hand, incredulous, flexing my digits in horror.

The human must have felt the difference in my alarm, for he focused his gaze on me. "What did I do?"

I did not answer—could not. I had to know.

I reached my hand forward to touch the force field, aware it had been set to repel.

A searing arc of electrical discharge coursed through my hand, and the prisoner gasped, staring down at his own hand, experiencing a shock that mirrored mine.

NINE

"So much for professional detachment," I muttered, when I came to my senses.

I collected myself—or rather, I waited for sense of horror to dissipate, unable to wrap my mind around the truth. For it simply could not be true.

Yet it was.

Or at least, it appeared to be.

What in the blazes are you rambling on about, the human asked me, seemingly irritated, but I felt the concern in his voice.

Concern that should not be there, and would normally not exist between an interrogator and their prisoner. Especially in this short amount of time.

I issued the command to deactivate the force field and strode toward him. "Is your hand stinging?" I asked him out loud, raising my mental shields reflexively, unwilling to look into his mind to find out the answer for myself. Not now that I knew...

"What?" he asked, exasperated, still able to read my thoughts which only confirmed my suspicion. "What do you know? You are more enigmatic than those damned Vorlons," he added.

"Is your hand stinging?" I repeated.

"Yes. What did you do to me?" he asked. "Is this some new mental voodoo crap?"

I did not answer for a very long time, but I could not escape the truth forever.

"We are a life-pairing," I told him, eventually, managing to keep my voice reasonably calm.

He took even longer to respond. "I am your...mate?"

"Yes," I replied, simply. "That is why we feel each other's pain."

I had expected horror, maybe even disgust, but instead I felt...relief?

"I thought I was going insane, Greenie," he explained, quietly.

I followed his thoughts. "Your people do not usually exhibit such strong mental abilities, do they?"

"No," he confirmed. "It's a new evolutionary ability, and spotty at best."

"So our unique...connection must have amplified it, somehow."

I suddenly felt vulnerable, and very, *very* self-conscious. I had a mate. It should be a joyous occasion—something to treasure, literally, for the rest of my life—but all I could think of was: *what do we do now? There is no way my people will accept you—accept us. Maybe my pod-siblings would—or at least Reymeen, eventually—but I do not have too much pride to say that my species, as a whole, would be equally prejudiced about "something different" than your ancestors were.*

Well, at least we're more alike than we knew at first glance, he teased, also switching to the more intimate form of communication that had grown so naturally between us. *And to answer your question, perhaps we start by you finally acknowledging that I have a name. If I'm referred to as "the prisoner," "the alien," or "the human" for too much longer I will need to suggest we go to marriage counseling.*

I should not be surprised he would try to make light of a serious situation, to try and lesson the acute stress and shock we both were feeling while adjusting to our new reality, but I found I also agreed with him; I no longer saw him as my prisoner.

How could I?

I am known to my family, and my close friends, as Chip, he suggested, helpfully.

But that is not even your name.

Not the one I was given at birth…but it is a known nickname for Forrest.

Somehow it did not feel right. *You call me Greenie*, I pointed out, *presumably for my skin coloration.*

Yes, he replied, *but I do* not, *by any stretch of the imagination, want you calling me Pinkie, for the base color of mine.*

Why not? I asked, genuinely curious. *Is it still an insult in your culture to differentiate between the contrasting skin colors of your races?*

Oh, god no, he replied. *It's just not…manly.*

Then how about I call you Brown. Not for your skin color, but—

I get it, he interrupted. *And the symmetry is appropriate, I suppose….*

We looked at each other for a long, awkward moment, at a loss at what to talk about next.

I have so many questions, Brown said, finally.

So did I. Foremost among them: *How is this possible?*

I was just about to ask you the same thing.

I did not have the answers, but I knew someone who should. Several someones.

We needed to talk to a Psych Healer.

Wasn't the imbecile that had supposedly sedated your sister—in an attempt to treat her—one of those so-called "Psych Healers?" My bruised windpipe remembers that doc's failure all too well.

That was an exceptional circumstance, I replied, in the Psych Healer's defense.

And what are we?

I blinked. He had a point. *It is the only option we have*, I told him, a little desperate. I felt the stress start to build again, the fear return. *Who are we fooling? We cannot be paired—it will cause too many complications. We could never be physically apart again, for instance, and how will that work when…*

We'll work it out, Greenie, Brown interrupted me. He hesitated, then I felt a warm, soothing mental caress calming my nerves. *So, what now?* he asked, back to business.

Follow me, I replied.

We had made it out of the cell, down the corridor, and to the main exit of the Interrogation block when we were suddenly surrounded by armed guards. In my shock and confusion, I had forgotten to alert my unit as to my actions.

Put your weapons down, I ordered, angry with myself, not them. They were simply doing their jobs, something I was clearly incapable of doing—would *not* do. *I will not lose my mate.*

I felt Reymeen's shock at that last statement, and the guards parted to let him through.

Keelarah, have you lost leave of your senses? He is a prisoner, an alien…

I know all of this, I told him, in as firm a voice as I could assemble. *But he is in need of medical attention. We* both *are.*

I was suddenly grabbed from behind and pulled back, away from Brown.

He whirled, instinctively leaping to my defense.

No, stay where you are, I warned him, but he took no heed.

He reached for me and Reymeen ordered the guards to shoot, blue-green electrical bolts surrounded his body, coursing through his neural pathways, paralyzing the electrical center of his brain.

I told them to stop, tried to intervene, but betraying hands held me back.

The pain intensified, his frame becoming rigid until it shuddered uncontrollably; I felt the agony he was suffering as if it were my own.

A piercing scream filled the room.

I had just enough awareness to see our captors turn to look at me in shock before everything went black.

TEN

I woke up disoriented, my body shaking. *Brown!*

I am here, Greenie, he replied, sending a warm, gentle caress to sooth my mind. *Am fending off these blasted B.U.G.s again.*

Confused, I tried to sit up, only to discover my head was strapped into some kind of neuromonitor.

Are you okay? he asked, his mental voice reflecting the pain he was trying so hard to suppress.

I sent him an affirmative, and opened my eyes to see the preeminent Psych Healer, Porleeni, talking to Reymeen and two of the highest-ranking officers in the Cartheeli Military Caste. I started to panic.

I have been treated fairly, Brown reassured me. *My leg is still missing in action, however.*

I recognized what he was doing—putting on a facade of bravado and humor to help calm me, or himself—but he must have known our position was precarious. Even though he was my mate, in a way I had betrayed my pod, my caste and species, just from the inherent implications of our...union. That would not be easily understood.

A comforting warmth filled my mind. *Your heart was in the right place. Hopefully you can convince them of that.*

No one should be able to hear a soul-pairing's conversation, yet I "felt" the Psych Healer react to his words.

I focused my gaze on what she was studying: a holographic Bioscan of the alien. No surprise there. They had hurt him. We were obviously in the Medilab again and—

Then I saw it: a thin, almost ethereal thread emanating out of the three-dimensional image of Brown's skull, stretching across into…the Bioscan image of a Cartheeli skull!

My skull.

Brown felt my shock and surged deeper into my mind, trying to comprehend what I was seeing. I watched, fascinated, as the silver thread brightened and pulsed in response to his action, and I felt him turn to study the holographic display himself.

"They are a soul-pairing!" Porleeni announced, her tone more than a little incredulous as she looked at the iridescent thread connecting our minds.

I felt my pod-brother's surprise as everyone else in the room fixed their gaze on the irrefutable evidence.

While I had known it, felt it, *seeing* the connection between our minds added a whole new level of realization. I did not understand how the Bioscan could show our spiritual bond, but the device had been detecting life-pairings for countless generations.

"How is this possible?" Reymeen asked the Psych Healer, horrified.

"How can we…undo it?" added Boorlath, the Supreme Commander of the Cartheeli Caste.

"To forcibly remove the bond would kill them both," Porleeni asserted.

Much to my surprise, the thought of losing my partner petrified me.

"But it cannot be a true bond!" the other officer insisted, disgust coloring his tone. "I mean…he is…."

"What?"

"An *alien!*" he spluttered, like the word itself was an insult.

I reached out to my pod-brother to appeal to him for help, only to find he had closed off his mind to me, shutting the door on my only avenue of support. The betrayal stung.

"How could you betray us like this?" the Supreme Commander demanded, echoing my thoughts.

I felt Brown's indignation, an instinctive flaring of that protective nature I was growing to love, and was fascinated to see the corresponding flare of intensity in the silver thread connecting us. *It will be better for us both if I handle this*, I told him, sending him an apologetic caress.

"I did not *choose* this bond," I pointed out. "Neither did Prisoner Brown. We had simply wanted to escape its consequence."

That last line gave my pod-brother pause. "The connection might not have been your choice," he agreed, "but you *chose* to aid him instead of talking to me, instead of reporting the…his…incursion."

Incursion? Brown muttered darkly into my mind. *It's like they think I'm a bloody parasite.*

"I wanted my mate to survive," I replied simply. "No, I *needed* him to survive. Everyone here has either witnessed or experienced how irrevocable the connection is between soulpairings, how impossible it is to be apart for too long."

"But he is an alien," the second officer pointed out, again.

"Yes, we have established that," I replied, exasperated.

"What I mean is…the soul-pairing should not have been possible. His anatomy is completely different—"

"On a physical level, that is—at least visually—an accurate observation," Porleeni interrupted, with all her expertise as Psych Healer, "but both species' brains are built in a similar manner, relying on a central nervous system and a certain biochemical balance to conduct thought and action throughout the body. And, based on Keelarah's reports, both of our species also exhibit a remarkably similar mental ability to project and receive thought and emotions."

"You cannot be saying we have a psychological compatibility to this…this prisoner," the Supreme Commander insisted.

Porleeni inclined her head. "That is indeed what I am saying. Furthermore, while I have no prior medical history to ascertain whether the human's physical form is undergoing some type of metamorphosis, analysis of Keelarah's Bioscans confirm she is going through subtle physiological changes to accommodate a soul-pairing with a member of an alien species."

"Are you saying that bonding with me triggered human-like changes to her genetic profile?" Brown asked, our shock evident in his voice.

"That is an oversimplification, but yes, it would appear—"

"—that perhaps you have discovered physical proof that the prisoner has subverted our Lead Interrogator to his cause," the Supreme Commander insisted.

"No, that is not what I said," Porleeni corrected him, her tone firm. "Extensive studies have proven that there is no conscious decision that goes into the process of developing a soul-pairing. While the profound differences in their anatomy will ensure they can never physically mate, these two will presumably go through more physiological changes than the usual soul-pairing as they complete their bond. In my professional assessment you need to factor in their emotional vulnerability at the creation of this unusual life-pairing when you form judgments on their recent actions. They are—quite literally—not in their right minds as they go through this transitional phase."

"I think it is abhorrent that we are considering this…this…partnership to be akin to a true life-pairing," the second officer interjected. "I do not care what those bioscans show. The alien used his mind-bending tricks to somehow manipulate the Lead Interrogator into betraying her caste. The only thing we should be discussing now is a suitable punishment."

Brown reached up to his Neuromonitor, yanking it off his head so he could sit up in his Medicapsule. "In an ideal universe I would have found a way to escape and contact the nearest Human ship without any assistance, having no compunction about revealing the location of your secret base to my people if it meant I could have been rescued earlier." He raised his hands to stall any protests. "You have to understand, as a prisoner I have no reason to feel loyalty toward you, and I certainly wouldn't have cared if I never saw any of you again."

No offense, he added privately.

None felt, I replied.

"Except," Brown continued, "and here is the important part: I now have a genuine bond with Keelarah. I not only *want* to protect her, but I have a *compulsion* to do so; it is like I have imprinted on her. Even if you set me free today, I know I can't return to my home planet if Keelarah wants to stay here. I know that I *need* to be with her; that it literally hurts if we are physically too far apart. If that is not a life-pairing, I don't know what the hell it is."

The Supreme Commander considered him, and his words, for a long moment. "You could be loyal to her, but the side effects of a life-pairing does not inherently make you trust-worthy to *us*."

I opened my mouth to reply, but Brown silenced me. *I've got this, Greenie.*

"I'll concede that point," he agreed, "but from my under-standing of all this, doesn't the bond ensure that I am physi-cally—emotionally—incapable of betraying her? And if so...."

Interest flared in the Supreme Commander's eyes. "And so you believe that proves to us we should trust you not to hurt or deceive the rest of us, because doing so would be betraying her?"

"Exactly."

An odd expression passed over the second officer's face and before I could protest or his superior could order him to desist, he muttered, "We shall see," and advanced on me, gripping my hand so hard within his that I felt a bone crack.

The Psych Healer protested vehemently, but Brown's reac-tion was much more decisive. Without thought for the conse-quences he sent a violent mental blast that rendered the officer unconscious within seconds.

"Don't worry, he'll live," Brown muttered through gritted teeth.

"How long have you had that ability?" the Supreme Com-mander demanded, more incredulous than angry.

Brown winced, flexing his hand as if it hurt too. "Since I met and bonded with Keelarah. My telepathic abilities were never that strong, that consistent, before her...before us."

You should have let the others intervene, I told him, wavering between concern and exasperation.

I honestly had no idea I was going to have such an effect on him, he replied. *I had only wanted to "push" him away from you, not into a coma.*

"You could have killed him," Boorlath pressed, as if he had heard Brown's thought.

And maybe he did. That man was an enigma encased in a uniform. I was never quite sure what he was capable of.

"Yes," Brown replied, crushing another B.U.G. that had been buzzing around his torso. He locked gazes with the Supreme Commander.

"Did you *want* to? Answer me true."

I felt a surge of protectiveness, as Brown looked over to see the Psych Healer work on repairing my hand. "In that moment, yes."

"You have your proof now," Reymeen stated quietly, reminding everyone he was still in the room. "He cannot be trusted."

"He acted to *protect* me, not betray me," I pointed out, as I watched Porleeni move to check the officer over. "Surely that distinction is important."

"While we can no longer dispute the truth of the soul-pairing," the Supreme Commander admitted, "and we acknowledge that neither of you *chose* to be bonded, I cannot see how we transition to accept a prisoner—specifically an *alien* of such volatile abilities—into our society."

"I can teach him how to control his powers," I suggested, a little desperately.

"Yes, that could indeed be true," Boorlath agreed, "but I have my doubts as to the stability of your pairing. Even if we could grow to trust him, the simple fact is it was *your* decision to release the prisoner without seeking authorization from the chain of command, *your* decision to aid him over the good of your people. How can we publicly endorse your actions, while

I am still struggling to understand them myself?" He hesitated, then continued. "We cannot easily get past how much this life-pairing has already changed you, inside and out."

"Doesn't your race have a thing called forgiveness?" Brown asked, aggravated on my behalf. "It's not Keelarah's fault I landed on your planet and turned her life upside down."

"No, it is not," my pod-brother agreed, turning to look at me with infinite sadness, a finality to his tone. "But this is so *unnatural*."

The words hung heavy in the air.

I tore my gaze away to look at Brown, realizing that the conversation was no longer about whether the human belonged, or whether our soul-pairing should be validated, or even accepted. For I now knew that *I* was the one who was being told I no longer belonged. In the process of finding my life partner—in discovering the connection that should have been the biggest joy of my life—I had become an alien in the eyes of my species.

ELEVEN

The room was small, cold. Too gray for my liking, but I did not have a choice in the matter.

Gone were the bio-organic walls, and the peaceful hums of the sentient plants I had taken for granted my whole life.

I turned around, taking in the stark, harsh lines of the enclosed space I now called home, and cringed. The only redeeming feature—my one connection to the privileged life I had once lived—was that my personal sleeping pod had been integrated into this stark cell of a room.

Now I knew what it felt to be a prisoner.

A deep-sounding chuckle filled my mind. *It can't be as bad as all that, can it, Greenie?*

He was right. It could have been a whole lot worse.

There you go, Brown replied. *Keep up that positive spirit.*

I sent him a partly-disapproving, mostly-playful mental slap, and heard his laugh again, except this time the sound was closer. My ears had heard it, too.

The door to my right slid open with a whoosh, and my lifemate floated in on his gravity neutralizer, pulling his mouth into that now-familiar position that exposed his teeth. "How do you like your humble abode?" he asked.

"'Like' is not an adequate word to describe it," I replied.

He laughed again, but then his expression sobered. "I hope eventually the *Wanderer* can feel like home to you."

I felt his concern, and softened. "I am sure it will. I do not want to appear ungrateful—"

"—but because of me you'll have to leave everything you ever knew—all that you ever loved—to fly in this small tin bucket. I get it, I truly do."

It had taken several days for the Supreme Commander of the Cartheeli Military Caste to decide what should be done with us. In light of our recent soul-pairing, and the unusual physiological adaptations my body had undergone to acclimate to an alien life-mate, my actions were deemed something akin to a psychotic break. In truth, they had no way of knowing how much I would change through sharing my soul with something *Other*, because the bond was still new and strengthening. All they knew is that prior to my soul-pairing, I had had an exemplary record, and they had to take that into account.

So what to do with me? They could not endorse my recent actions, as Lead Interrogator of the Neuropsych Unit, but there were medical reports that showed what had triggered them.

They decided on the most *humane* (oh, how I loved that word!) option available to them. I would be pardoned, providing I never set foot on Cartheelian soil ever again.

The thought of never talking to my people again—and most importantly my pod-siblings—nearly tore me apart; it was all Brown could do to hold me together, in the days that had followed the pronouncement.

But there was also some good to come out of their decision: they could not keep Brown incarcerated if I had to leave our planetary system. Even the harshest punishment our courts could deliver fell short of execution, due to the very real possibility that the criminal's death could mentally shatter his surviving life-mate. They knew the separation alone could kill us, especially at this vulnerable stage of bonding, so he had been exiled alongside me.

Asteroid Miner brats are not easy to kill, Brown pointed out, *although I would prefer that we not test my mortality for a third time this year.*

I felt his curiosity and watched him as glided over to my pod, hesitating when he got close to it.

"You can touch it, if you want," I invited.

He reached out a five-fingered hand and gently rested it against the pulsating outer shell of the pod.

Fascinated, I saw the iridescent blue-green threads of light flow towards his hand, pulsating directly underneath it as it analyzed my mate. The contrast between the ethereal luminescence of the pod and his tanned skin was rather striking.

He turned to me with wide eyes. "It's...*whispering* to me!" he exclaimed.

"Yes," I said. "It is a living organism."

"I thought it was simply a sleeping capsule—a way for you to get sustenance."

"You are correct, but it is also organic. It grew *with* me, absorbing my essence. I sustain it as much as it sustains me."

"It's now...*rubbing* me!" he announced, mesmerized.

"Its function is to soothe and nurture," I replied. "It recognizes you as my mate."

I felt his surprise, and then he did something I never expected. He directed an empathetic burst of warmth and welcome into the pod, rubbing its surface gently with his hand.

The response was electric—literally. The pulsing lights quickened, and it was as if the pod hummed.

Finally, reluctantly, he pulled his hand back, moving back far enough so he could study how the pod had been retrofitted so that its vine-like appendages could be wired into his ship's circuitry. "Will it become part of the ship?" he asked, eventually.

It was my turn to be surprised. "You are perceptive. I have no way of knowing for certain—this is new territory for both of us, and our technologies—but I suspect it will slowly integrate itself with *Wanderer's* systems as it grows used to its new environment, and adapts."

I wondered if that would bother him. I had already complicated his life enough, without messing with his beloved vessel.

He turned back to lock his gaze with mine. *It's going through the physical process our souls have already gone through—are going through—to better integrate our lives. There is something...poetic about that.*

I wanted to reply, but halted, feeling a polite "knock" on the surface level of my mind. "Brown, we need to go to the Control Room."

"Visitor?" he asked.

"Yes," I replied simply, anxiety dominating my emotional bandwidth.

We left my new pod-room, a cumbersome process for me, because the ship had not built for three-legged species. It had not been built for one-legged species, either, but Brown's Gravity Neutralizer helped him bypass the "rung ladder" that took us up to the Operational Level of the ship. Me, I had to dangle one leg awkwardly behind me, as the other two struggled to clamber up the metal rungs.

By the time we had made it to the Control Room, I was out of breath, and Brown was out of patience.

"Stop messing with my ship," he ordered, when he saw six-digit hands playing with wires behind a wall panel. Their owner had the grace to project shame, before replacing the transparent casing and turning around.

"Reymeen!" I exclaimed.

"I can see the integration process has started," he said quietly, by way of greeting, and I noticed that iridescent bio-organic strands had now reached the circuitry powering the Control Room, interweaving in and around the ship's various power boards.

"I did not think I would see you again," I stated.

"I did not think I *could* see you again," he replied.

I tried not to show how much his words hurt, but he had opened his mind to me again; it was inevitable.

Warmth surged into my mind, shadowed by an intense impression of guilt. *I was...disgusted*, he told me on our private link. *I did not want to feel that way, but the revelation of your… union…awoke prejudices I was not aware I had harbored. I could not…no, I* would not, *subject you to them.*

That was why you had closed your mind to me? I asked. *You did not want to hurt me?*

Of course! My thoughts were abhorrent, even to me. It felt as if you had betrayed me, but my reaction was unforgiveable.

I closed my eyes, my relief palpable, even to Brown, who was not privy to our conversation. I felt my life-mate relax and prepare the ship for launch, so I focused my full attention on my brother. *I am the one who should apologize. I had thought it would be easy for you to accept us, because we are pod-siblings. I should have realized it would make it* harder *for you to accept us, because you would be more personally affected by the changes this life-pairing had wrought on me. If I had known what you were feeling, I could have reassured you…explained…*

It was Reymeen's turn to express relief, intermingled with sadness. *You have been cleared for takeoff,* he suddenly announced.

I turned around to see Brown activating monitors. *This is really happening, then,* I replied, finally realizing how divergent our paths would become.

I will miss you, sister of my soul.

And I you, I replied, turning back around to discover my pod-brother was no longer in the Control Room, no longer in my mind.

I turned to see Brown's warm eyes considering me. "Ready?" he asked.

"No," I replied, simply, "but let us go anyway."

He walked over to me, and reached for one of my hands, interweaving his five digits with the six of mine, his grip sure, warm.

Comforting.

He turned us toward the viewscreen, to all possibilities along the horizon. "Where to?"

I reached my other hand out to rest it on the console in front of me, both of us surprised to see it activate; it already recognized my touch.

"Away," I announced simply, and the *Wanderer* launched for the stars.

WHEN PARALLEL LINES MEET

BOOK TWO

GOLDEN DREAM

MIKE RESNICK

ONE

I waited until we were sure there was no pursuit, then turned to Keelarah.

"Time to pull the star charts up on this thing, Greenie," I said.

"Why?" she said. "We're headed for Earth."

"I didn't want to argue with you when I was all but helpless," I replied, "but there's got to be two dozen worlds, some of them human, some not, that can fit me out with a new leg in far less time that it would take to get to Earth, even if we were going there."

"We're not?" she asked.

I shook my head, then realized that she probably didn't know what the gesture meant. "My race was born there, but we're living on a few dozen worlds now, and most of them have had more experience with alien races."

"But—"

"You really want to spend a few months in jail while I explain that you, Keelarah, the enemy's Chief Interrogator—yeah, I know you're not the enemy, but it'll take some time to convince them—mean us no harm and actually broke me out of that hellhole?"

"You are speaking of *my* world," she said harshly.

"I am speaking of *my* prison cell on your world," I replied. "Anyway, maybe they'd believe me, but the odds are they won't, and I've no intention of being the reason that you get to sample *our* version of alien incarceration."

She seemed about to argue, and then she suddenly went limp—well, as limp as a fully awake person can be when sitting in one of those damned uncomfortable chairs; uncomfortable for humans, anyway—and nodded her head. I didn't think it was a natural gesture of her race, but she'd seen me do it often enough and picked it up from her constant proximity to me.

"Okay," I continued. "Let's bring up the charts."

I gave the ship an order and a holographic cube, about four feet on a side, suddenly appeared above and to the right of the control panel. Each star and planet had a small, flashing logo giving its name and various other things—gravity and atmospheric content, I assumed—that I couldn't read.

"Shit!" I muttered.

"Oh," she said. "They seem to have reprogrammed it for Cartheeli while you were in captivity."

"I don't read Cartheeli, of course," I replied. "Hell, I only read two or three human languages."

"Which ones?" she asked.

"You have a reason for asking?" I said.

"Of course."

"Terran, Vandolian, and a bit of Carmalite."

She addressed the control panel in her native tongue. It responded, she gave it a quick comment, and then turned to me with a smile.

"Look," she said.

"I *am* looking," I replied.

She smiled again. "Not at *me*. At the map."

I looked at the cube, and sure enough, every word that had been a mystery to me a minute earlier now appeared in Vandolian.

"Smarter ship than I thought it was," I said, studying the map.

"Ships aren't smart or stupid," she corrected me. "It had a smart programmer—or *re*programmer."

I studied the map in silence for a few minutes.

"It's off to the right," she said. "Or if you prefer, Galactic Southeast."

"What are you talking about?" I asked.

"Vandolia," she said. "You speak it, so I assume it's a human colony world."

"It's a human military outpost," I corrected her.

"But—"

"I speak it because I grew up there, but by the same token, I'm not taking us to a military world where they'll be inclined to do to you what your people did to me."

It was beyond strange. I was speaking in Terran, she was speaking in her own tongue, but because of this *link* we understood each other perfectly.

"Even if you vouch for me?" she asked.

I shrugged, a gesture that was probably lost on her. "It depends on how recently they've been attacked, and by who."

"You make it sound like all you do is fight wars," she said disapprovingly.

"Actually, very few of us do, compared to the size of our entire civilization, and those who do tend to do it very reluctantly."

"It still seems warlike to me," said Keelarah.

"So says the member in good standing of the Cartheeli Military," I replied with a wry smile.

"We exist to defend our race!" she said heatedly.

"Do you find it that hard to believe the same of us?" I asked. "I think I'm the first member of my race you've ever met."

"I am sorry," she said. "I meant no insult. It's just that the first time I probed your mind, there was such anger and hatred there…"

"You mean right after you blew my leg off and incarcerated me?" I suggested.

"It was a first impression," she said. "A strong one, but a wrong one. I apologize if I have offended you."

"I'm the one who should apologize to you," I said. I gently patted the stump of my leg. "*My* war is over. But you are leaving behind everyone and everything you ever knew."

"I'm not at war," she said.

"Neither am I," I said.

"Then what are we?" she wondered aloud.

"Two lost souls," I said with a sad smile. Sad for our present, and sad for our likely future, where one or both of us figured to be shunned by just about every race we came in contact with.

And that was if we were lucky.

TWO

"Okay, Ship," I said. "Find me a planet with an atmosphere and gravity both of us can breathe and function in."

"I do not breathe, and therefore do not require atmosphere," replied the ship.

"I meant *her* and me. And make sure it's not at war with anyone, and not part of any military empire."

"This could take some time," said the ship.

"Just do it before we run out of food and air."

"Yes, sir."

"And my name is Chip."

"I still do not quite understand this 'nickname' thing. I thought your name was Forrest," said Keelarah.

"It's Chip to my friends," I said. She frowned, and I added: "Consider it an energy-saving name. One less syllable to pronounce."

She stared at me for a long moment. "That is a joke, correct?"

I nodded. "The best jokes usually have a little truth hanging around the edges."

"You don't mind if I still call you by your last name, Brown, do you? It just…fits better."

I shrugged. "Go for it."

"I am getting hungry," she said. "Do you mind if I eat?"

"Be my guest."

"I am not your guest," she said. Then she saw the expression on my face. "Oh. That is another joke?"

"Not if you don't at least smile at it," I answered. "Go ahead and eat."

"Would you like something, too?"

"Not just yet," I said.

"But you haven't eaten in more than a day."

"I'm waiting for a better chef," I said. "Or at least a better menu."

"What is a chef?" she asked.

"Never mind. Just believe me that, with no insult intended, your world's food is not the tastiest I've ever encountered."

"But it has kept you alive," she said defensively.

"True," I admitted. "And when I get desperate enough, it'll keep me alive again." I smiled. "But I'm not quite that desperate yet."

"Chip," said the ship, "I have found three worlds that fit your description."

"Choose the one with the lightest gravity and head toward it," I replied.

"Why the lightest gravity?" asked Keelarah.

"Because wherever we land I'm going to have them fit me up with an artificial leg, and since it's not a human planet, I'm sure they haven't performed this surgery to the point where it's old hat to them, and if I'm going to fall down a bunch of times while I'm learning to locomote with whatever they give me, I'd rather do it on a low gravity world."

"What do hats have to do with it?" she repeated, frowning in confusion.

"Slang," I said.

"Maybe if we just communicated via the psychic link, I wouldn't be so befuddled," said Keelarah.

"I couldn't keep you out of my brain if I wanted to," I told her. "I don't feel at all uncomfortable knowing you're there, and the connection became useful when I was imprisoned. But until I get more used to it, I'll continue speaking aloud. It's the way I've communicated since I was born."

"Understood," she said.

"Chip," said the ship, "I have checked, and none of the major population centers speak Terran, Valdolian, or Carmalite."

"We'll just have to make do," I said.

"Do?" replied the ship. "What is do, and how does one make it?"

"Slang," I said yet again. "I mean we'll just have to deal with the conditions that exist." I thought for a moment. "Are they a neutral world, open to visitors and tourists, or a closed world?"

"If they were a closed world I would have been warned off when I obtained the planetary readings."

"What language did they use to give you the readings?"

"It was entirely mathematical."

I was going to bemoan the fact that I didn't speak Calculus, but then it occurred to me that I'd have to explain or excuse it, and I was getting a little tired of both.

"Has the planet got a name?" I asked.

"I do not know."

"Ask it."

"In what language, Chip?"

"Try Terran," I said. "If they've ever had any Terran visitors, they may have the language programmed into the spaceport, even if no one else knows or speaks it."

"Yes, Chip," said the ship.

"Yes, they speak it?" I said, surprised it had found out so quickly.

"Yes, Chip, I shall try Terran, though I like all the new languages I've learned at the Cartheeli Base better."

"Great. On top of everything else, my love life is corrupting military issue hardware."

"I am not corrupted," replied the ship.

"My mistake," I said. "Just contact the planet."

"Yes, Chip."

There was a momentary silence.

"Yes, Chip."

"You said that already."

"Yes, Chip, the spaceport can communicate in Terran."

"Good!" I said. "Can you give me a visual?"

"Of the planet?" replied the ship. "You already have it."

"No, I mean of one of the inhabitants."

"Is there any inhabitant in particular you wish to see?"

"Whoever you've been talking to," I said, trying to control my temper.

"But I have not spoken to an inhabitant, but a spaceport computer."

"Just show me what a resident looks like and don't hassle me, okay?" I said.

"Yes, Chip," said the ship.

A moment later something out of a child's nightmare appeared on the viewscreen. It was massive, with rolls of flab—or at least flesh—slopping down over dozens of other rolls that were all doing the same thing. It had two...well, I want to call them arms, but they were boneless appendages, very much akin to tentacles, except that they ended in a series of bristles that seemed to function as fingers.

It had two eyes, two ears (or, rather, earholes), and a broad mouth. There was no nose, and I wondered how it could breathe when it was eating or speaking...and then I saw a couple of, not noses, but breathing orifices in its neck.

I noticed Keelarah staring at the screen in rapt fascination.

"You've seen them before?" I asked.

She shook her head. "Never. They are very...*unusual*...aren't they?"

"I'm sure you've seen stranger," I said.

"Yes," she answered. "But always under controlled circumstances, such as prison cells or even peace conferences. I have never met any race that looks remotely like this, alone and unarmed, on its home world."

"No sense bringing along a weapon. You'll never get it past Security or Customs." I paused. "Always assuming they *have* Security or Customs."

She stared at me for a long minute. "And you really want these people—and I use the word advisedly—to work on your leg?"

"Nobody's working on my leg," I said, still staring at the screen.

"But I thought..." she began.

"My leg is a distant memory," I said. "I want them to work on an *artificial* leg and attach it so that it functions as a leg."

"Can you not wait until we can find a race whose appearance is more...more...?" She searched for a word.

"More normal?" I suggested.

"Exactly!" she exclaimed.

"I am a soldier who hunts for alien worlds to conquer them. You are an inquisitor who deals with aliens your race has captured, theoretically because they meant to harm you. Who is to say that these plug-uglies aren't friendlier and more helpful than either of our races?"

"So you insist on landing there?"

"First I insist on finding out if they consider us an enemy," I said. "Then I insist on finding out if they can fix me up with a workable leg. If we aren't enemies and they've got a doctor or mechanic who can get me walking again, then yes, I insist on landing here."

She just stared at me and made a little gesture with her left arm, which I assumed was her version of a shrug.

"Okay, Ship," I said, "ask them if they have anyone who speaks Terran or Valdolian."

"What about Carmalite?" asked the ship. "You mentioned before that you can speak it."

"Not without difficulty, and if they're going to mess with my stump I want to make sure I understand every word."

"Understood," said the ship. A moment later its voice came back on. "None of them speak Terran or Valdolian, but they do have a translating mechanism that many of them carry that can translate Terran into their tongue and vice versa."

"Good," I said. "What's the name of this dirtball, by the way?"

"Elgram IV," said the ship.

"So the star is Elgram?"

"Translated into Terran," explained the ship.

"Fine," I said. "Now tell them that your pilot wants to converse with someone in authority, and stress that they have to activate their translating mechanism, as I don't possess one up here."

"You possess the ship," said Keelarah.

"It makes no difference. I can't imagine they're going to come aboard with all the equipment they need to give me a new leg, so at some point I will have to leave the ship and enter their equivalent of a medical facility."

"Or a scientific one," she said. "After all, you want an *artificial* leg."

"It just has to get me from one place to another," I said. "My dancing days are over, Greenie."

"What is dancing?" asked Keelarah.

"It's where a male and a female hold each other…"

"You mean like a hug?"

"Kind of like a hug," I said. "But only from the waist up. The couple's feet move in artistic patterns in time with the music. Different music requires different forms of dancing." *And anything a singer can scream to requires you to have a drink and sit that one out.*

"It sounds interesting," said Keelarah, and I could tell she meant it.

"Chip," interrupted the ship, "the entities on the planet want to know if we intend to land."

"Before we do anything else," said Keelarah to the ship, "find out exactly what the gravity and atmosphere are, and also the temperature." She turned to me with her equivalent of a smile. "There are worlds with atmospheric conditions identical to mine, but the mean temperature is"—she paused for a moment, translating it into figures I could understand—"halfway between what you consider normal and absolute zero, and others are almost hot enough to spontaneously burst into flame."

"You heard her, Ship," I said. "Get some answers, and translate them into Terran and Cartheeli."

"Yes, Chip," said the ship.

There was a moment of silence.

"Average gravity, 0.93 Standard, though of course Keelarah's Standard is completely different."

"Confusing, isn't it, having two races' Standards to cope with?" interjected Keelarah.

"Yes, it is," replied the ship. "Atmosphere is somewhat richer than normal, oxygen content up seven percent, nitrogen content down five percent, inert elements—"

"Just a minute," I said. "I assume that's Earth Normal and Earth Standard. I wasn't born on Earth, and in fact I've been there only once, for about a week."

"Your species has not evolved to the point where Earth's atmosphere and gravity would prove deleterious to your health," replied the ship, "and it is the practice through this segment of the galaxy to describe planetary details in terms of where the questioning race originated."

I nodded my head. "Makes sense at that," I said. "Now that I know the planetary conditions won't kill me, let me make sure we can say the same about their medical profession. Tell them that I want to speak to someone in authority who can arrange surgery on an alien being."

"Yes, Chip," said the ship.

A moment later another blob-like creature appeared on the viewing screen.

"I am Kzanos," it said.

"I am Forrest Brown. I believe the ship has identified my race for you."

"Within its limitations," came the answer.

"We come in peace," I said, "and I myself am in need of medical help."

"Oh?" said Kzanos.

"If you know my race or have reference to some description of it, you will know that we locomote on two legs."

"How awkward," said Kzanos, and I could almost detect a note of sympathy in his voice.

"My particular situation is even more awkward," I replied. "I am missing one of my legs."

His face began displaying different expressions, none of which made any sense to me. "Are you requesting that we help you look for it?"

"No," I said. "It was destroyed, and I need a replacement."

"Destroyed?" he repeated, making another face. "How?"

"An accident," I said. "The details are unimportant. What *is* important is that I get a functioning leg to replace it." I paused to let him digest that. "It needn't look like the leg I lost," I continued. "It just has to function as that leg did, because I am just about unable to locomote without it."

"And it makes no difference to you what it looks like?"

"Not as long as it works," I said.

"All right," said Kzanos. "Give us two solar days to study races with similar structures and biology to yours, and to determine the best material to use." A pause. "Are you immune to pain?"

"Absolutely not," I said.

He made a rumbling noise in his throat. "Make it three solar days," he said at last.

"Right," I said. "And thank you."

"Ending communication," he said, and suddenly the screen went black.

"Do not be afraid," said Keelarah. "I will be with you every minute."

"I'm already missing the damned leg," I replied. "I'll be more worried about you fainting than anything they can do to me."

"Faint?" she said, frowning. "Why would I faint?"

"If we're together long enough," I said, "I'm going to give you a sense of humor. That's a solemn pledge."

"Will it hurt?"

"I should hope not," I said.

She was still considering it when I hopped over to the galley to pour myself the equivalent of a cup of coffee an hour later.

THREE

Getting through Customs wasn't half the hassle I'd expected. They weren't at war with anyone, and they were used to visitors. I explained who we were, and they had a team of blobs (I never asked them what they called themselves) waiting for me. At first they wanted to take only me, but Keelarah objected.

"Are you sure?" I asked.

"Of course I'm sure," she replied. "We are psychically linked."

"I thought you couldn't be away from your sleeping pod too long," I replied, referring to the long translucent tube in the ship's small storage room. "Is there any way to…disentangle it from my ship to take it along?"

"That won't be necessary," she replied. "I can do just fine for a day or two. If they know what they're doing, that's all the time it should take. And if they don't know, we'll come right back to the ship."

"You're the boss," I said with a shrug. I wanted to say, "You're the captor" in the very same tone, but I remembered that she didn't have a fully developed sense of humor yet.

The vehicle seemed to face the wrong way, and two seats were hard as concrete, two were softer than down-filled pillows. The driver sat in his own enclosed compartment, which I'll swear didn't have a window in it. When the car (I call it a car, but there's never been a car anything like that) started moving, it traveled about a foot above the ground and still gave me the bumpiest ride I'd ever had.

As strange as the vehicle was, the layout of the city we cruised through was even stranger. Forty-story buildings stood next to tiny houses that couldn't hold more than two blobs, even if they'd just come over for a game of cards. Streets turned and curved onto themselves, there were no straight lines anywhere—not the streets, not the buildings, not even the directional signposts—and assuming our driver was obeying the speed limit, it went from a walk to a speedway and back to a walk again within almost every two-or-three-block area.

Finally we stopped—I almost said, "pulled up," but that would be a lie—and the doors slid back. We were near, though not quite in front of, a large building that I assumed was the hospital. Using my makeshift crutches I maneuvered around to the driver's compartment to ask him what we were expected to do next, but he began speeding off. I heard an angry shriek, and the vehicle almost did a backflip as it changed directions, pulled up to me, and let Keelarah out.

"You didn't wait for me," she said accusingly.

"How much effort does it take to keep up with a cripple?" I shot back.

Suddenly her expression changed. "I am so sorry, Brown," she said, and I thought I saw a tear, or her equivalent of one, running down her cheek. "I didn't think."

"Not a problem," I said, taking her hand and squeezing it gently. "If these bozos do their job, tomorrow you won't know any cripples. Or at least, not any human ones."

"Bozos?" she repeated. "Is that what the inhabitants call themselves?"

I smiled and shook my head. "That's what sardonic one-legged Earthmen call them when there's nobody here to meet us."

I looked at the building and tried to spot a door, or anything that passed for an entrance.

"Around the side, I think," said Keelarah.

"You see a door there?" I asked.

"No, but they have to be able to enter and exit with those huge bodies, and there *has* to be a door to accommodate them."

"Makes more sense than anything else in this damned city," I said. "Let's go take a look."

The left side of the building was covered with incomprehensible art by some blob who might have been Dali's or Picasso's soul brother, but there was no sign of an entrance. We walked totally around the building, and as we came back along the right side there was indeed a door wide enough to accommodate a couple of blobs walking side by side.

We entered, and the interior was as neat and orderly as the exterior of the building—and indeed the city—was crazed and illogical. There was a blob seated—or perhaps standing; they were pretty odd critters with so much flesh (or whatever it was) that one couldn't differentiate their legs if they weren't actually walking.

"May I help you?" said a mechanical voice.

It was the seated blob, and he/she/it spoke into an oddly-shaped mechanical instrument that was obviously the same kind of translator they'd used at the spaceport.

"You can't tell?" I said, leaning on my crutch.

"Are you the pilot the spaceport told us about?"

"Yes," I said, deciding not to argue whether I was a pilot or not.

"And you?" said the blob, turning to Keelarah.

"I am his...friend," she replied.

"You are not here to donate one of your limbs to him?"

I could tell she was about to give the blob an angry answer, and I didn't want her being forced to leave, so I interjected with a simple, "It wouldn't fit."

Thank you, said a voice inside my head. *I would have offended...her.*

Her? I thought back.

All right, him if you prefer. I just don't feel like referring to each of them as he/she/it.

Her it is, I thought and smiled at her. She returned the smile.

"I will need your name and planet of origin," said the blob, "as well as your race if you were not born on the planet where your race originated."

"My name is Forrest Brown," I answered. "My race is human, my planet of origin is Sapphire IV, and my race's planet of origin is Earth, which you may know as Sol III."

The blob seemed to be listening intently to an earpiece, though it was all but impossible to identify its ears. Finally it stared at me and its mouth contorted in what I hoped was a smile.

"You are a Man!" it said triumphantly. "And what remains of your uniform seems to state that you are in the military."

"Attached to it, anyway."

"And is this your prisoner?" it continued, indicating Keelarah. "Or perhaps a slave from some planet you conquered?"

"Her name is Keelarah, and she is a friend," I said. "And try to remember that I do not like it when my friends are insulted."

The blob gave me a look. I could almost hear the comment that went with it, in a tone of utter contempt: "Aren't you the touchy one?"

A moment later it spoke aloud and said, "We will remember," which made me wonder just how many blobs were listening to the conversation.

"Fine," I said. "Now, in case you haven't guessed, I need a leg."

"Actually," replied the blob, "that was precisely what I guessed."

"So direct me to a doctor and let's get busy," I said.

"I am a doctor."

"I thought you were a receptionist," I said.

"What is that?" asked the blob.

"A friendly doctor," interjected Keelarah before I could say something else insulting.

"Now," said the blob, staring at where my leg should have been, "you must understand that to create a fully functional leg of the type you are missing could take two to three years, perhaps half that time if we have some more Men to study."

"We haven't got that much time," I said. "How long to replace it with an artificial leg, something made of metal or some other sturdy substance?"

The blob considered my question for about forty seconds. Just when I was sure it had fallen asleep it spoke.

"We can replace it with a fully-functional artificial leg in something like six quaros."

I assumed a quaro was their equivalent of an hour, give or take.

"Okay," I said. "Let's do it."

"How do you plan to pay for this?" asked the blob.

"I have no currency with me," I said. "You'll have to perform an act of charity or trust me to pay you at a future date."

"That's what they all say," replied the blob.

"All?" I asked, frowning.

"All the wounded aliens," replied the blob. "We reconstruct hundreds of them. It comes from being a neutral world, I suppose."

"So will you do it?"

"Of course I will. The city pays me; your financial arrangements, or lack of same, are with them." The blob stood up. I'd say it got to its feet, but I still couldn't differentiate its feet from the rest of it. "I might as well get it done and send you and your slave on your way before dinnertime. No reason why I should delay or skip a meal because of an alien creature's missing appendage."

And so saying, it led Keelarah and me out of the reception area, down a corridor that wound as crazily as the streets did, and finally came to a room with seven walls, and a ceiling that varied in height from seven feet to perhaps eighteen feet, dependent (or so it seemed) on the mood of the architect.

The blob pointed to a surrealistic padded table that stood about six feet high.

"Lay down there," it said, indicating the table.

"If I could climb onto the goddamned table by myself, I wouldn't need another leg," I said.

"Oh," said the blob, as if the thought had never occurred to it. It turned to Keelarah. "Help your master onto the table."

Before I could object to the implication that she was a slave, she'd already half-lifted and half-pushed me up to the table.

"Oh, there's one question I should ask," said the blob.

"What?" I growled.

"Does your species have pain receptors?

"Do we *what?*"

"Can you feel pain?" it said.

"Hell, yes!" I snapped. "Didn't you get the memo from Spaceport?"

"Good," he said, reaching into his pocket, withdrawing a small bottle, and taking two pills from it. "Swallow them. They will make you sleep for the duration of the surgery, and will deaden any pain in the area for the next ten or fifteen *kaboes*."

I assumed a kaboe was a day. But it made no difference; I wasn't going to let anyone mess around with my still sore leg stump without some kind of pain medication. I swallowed the pills.

"I'm so glad I remembered," said the blob, as the pills took immediate effect and I started feeling drowsy. The last thing I heard before I fell asleep was, "You wouldn't believe how often they start shrieking if they feel any agony because I forgot to ask."

Keelarah held my hand, and that was the last thing I heard.

FOUR

I opened my eyes. I was lying on my back in the blob equivalent of a hospital bed.

"Well, that didn't take so long," I said.

"You've been asleep for a day and a night," said Keelarah, who was sitting across the room from me.

"That long?"

She nodded her head. "How do you feel?"

I frowned. "Not much different. Couldn't they do the surgery?"

"They did it."

I concentrated. "I can't feel a new leg down there."

"It's an artificial leg, created on the spot by a race that had probably never performed surgery on anything resembling a human before," she said. "It'll probably walk you from here to there, but I don't imagine they included any nerves or pair receptors that aren't absolutely essential for locomotion."

"Well, let's see," I said, sitting up and slinging my legs—one flesh and blood, one a thin metal shank ending in something that resembled a thick platter—over the side of the bed.

"Well?" she asked.

"It's about as ugly as legs get to be," I answered her. "From this moment on I will give up all thoughts of ever becoming a nudist, or playing any sport where the outfit includes short pants."

She shook her head. "I'm not asking about that. Does it *work?*"

"I suppose there's only one way to find out," I said.

I stood up. I still had no feeling in the leg, but I could feel the change in balance, which is to say I no longer felt like I was going to fall over on my side.

"Take a few steps," she suggested.

I frowned. "I don't know how to move the damned thing."

She pointed to a spot at the back of my head, just above the neck. "They did some minor surgery there. Maybe they attached…I don't know…for lack of a proper medical term, maybe they attached the equivalent of a control panel."

She walked over and offered me a shoulder to lean on.

I shook my head. "Go back to where you were," I said. "If you're right, I don't need you, and if you're wrong, I don't want to fall on you."

"You're sure?"

"I'm sure."

She offered what I had come to recognize as her equivalent of a shrug, and walked back to the far side of the room, though she didn't sit down again.

"All right," I said. "Here I go."

I thought about taking a step with my new left leg…and somehow it moved forward. Not smoothly. After all, it wasn't a human leg. But it moved, and I took another step with the good leg, then thought where I'd like my next step with my new leg to be and damned if it didn't go there, and a moment later I was walking around the room, first in a big circle, then in a figure-eight, then I even managed to back up a few steps.

"It feels all right?" she asked.

"I'll never be a track and field star, or win a beauty contest," I told her, "but yeah, it works and nothing hurts."

"I am very happy," she said.

"You and me both," I replied. "Hell, if you were a woman and I wound up marrying you, I'd call our first child Blob."

I chuckled at my remark, and I'd hoped she would too, but instead she looked seriously at me. "We cannot have a child, Brown."

"I know," I said with a sigh. "Hell, it's probably against thirty or forty laws for a man to marry an alien—or for a Cartheeli to marry what the Cartheelis consider an alien." I suddenly felt a little weak, so I sat back down on the bed. "Oh, well," I continued, "if I ever get a dog, I'll call *him* Blob."

"Someday we have to talk about that," said Keelarah.

"About dogs?" I asked. "They're four-legged carnivorous mammals, native to Earth, and—"

"No," she interrupted. "About a future in which neither of us can probably return to Cartheeli and will probably also not be welcome on Earth."

I shrugged. "That leaves only forty or fifty thousand worlds."

"How many would welcome both of us?"

I grimaced.

"Your leg?" she asked.

"No."

"Then what's bothering you?"

I offered her a wry smile. "I hate it when you ask questions like that."

"It's a serious consideration," said Keelarah.

"I know it is," I replied. "But let's handle one serious consideration at a time. A few weeks ago I was a prisoner on your planet. Now I'm not. Yesterday I had one leg; today I have two. We'll solve this one if it takes half a lifetime."

"I never asked," she said. "How long *is* your lifetime, and how much of it have you already lived?"

"Depends on which life you're talking about," I said.

She frowned. "I do not understand."

"One life ended, for all practical purposes, the day your people blew my leg away and captured me," I explained. "And my new life began the day I met you."

She dabbed at her eyes.

"I didn't know that Cartheeli could cry," I said.

She shot me a bittersweet smile. "Until today, I didn't know that either."

FIVE

We'd been traveling for two days when I decided it was time to land on a friendly or uninhabited planet—preferably a low-gravity one—and test out my leg. The ship was simply too small and cramped for me to know what it could and couldn't do, and given that the future was looking pretty uncertain, it was pretty important to get at least *some* answers.

I chose a water world, maybe eighty-five percent oceans and rivers and fifteen percent islands. There was nothing big enough to call a continent.

"Why here?" asked Keelarah as we touched down on a sandy beach.

"Are you aware of any militarily-aggressive starfaring races that evolved on water worlds?" I said.

"No."

I smiled. "Neither am I." I paused long enough for her to approximate a smile. "And since we're going to be on ship's rations until we set down permanently, I figure it can't hurt to add some fresh fish or whatever the hell lives in the water to our storage bins."

"You sound like you do this often."

"God forbid!" I said with a laugh. "There's a difference between being trained to survive alone while waiting for rescue or repairs and actually experiencing it."

"I've noticed you've used that word a few times," said Keelarah.

"Forbid?"

She shook her head. "God."

"Don't worry about it," I answered. "He never listens."

"I am assuming that God is your name for the deity."

"It's the most common one. We've got a few dozen others."

"Truly?" she asked.

"Truly," I replied. "There's God, and Jehovah, and Allah, and Ngai, and EnKai and YHWH, which is guaranteed to dislocate your jaw, and Elohim, and Baha, and—"

"You use them *all*?" she interrupted.

"*I* don't," I said. "But there are a few dozen religions in the Terran Confederation, and probably hundreds more among other races. It seems that most beings believe in a god; their religions and races just have different names for Him."

"As does mine," she said.

"What do you call him?"

She smiled. "You couldn't pronounce it."

"I'll just have to ignore Him then," I replied, "and settle for depending on myself."

"He is your god too," she said seriously. "He is everybody's god."

"If you say so."

She stared at me. "You don't believe in my god?"

I sighed deeply. "I don't believe in any of them." Then I smiled. "If they believe in me, that should be good enough."

"If our god were not protecting you, you would have died in captivity weeks ago."

"Then clearly my god is named Keelarah," I said.

"You must not say such a thing," she said seriously.

"Okay," I answered. "But you know I'm thinking it." The conversation was clearly causing her discomfort, so I decided it was time to test out the new leg. I checked the oxygen reading just to be on the safe side, and, doubtless thanks to all the water, it was an oxygen-rich atmosphere. No dangerous inert elements, and just enough other stuff that I wouldn't get high or drunk by taking a few deep breaths.

I hobbled to the hatch, but Keelarah got there first.

"Step aside," I said. "If I lose my balance I don't want to fall on you."

"I am going first," she said adamantly. "And if you lose your balance, I will catch or steady you." She paused, and then added, "For better or worse, we are a team."

I had no answer for that, so she climbed down to the ground and stood ready to catch or steady me if I started falling.

"There won't be a problem here," I said as I put my feet, one natural and artificial (I thought of them as one real and one phony) on the sand. "We know that I can walk a few steps around the ship." I pointed to a purple tree about eighty feet away. "Let's see if I can get there and back."

She nodded and began walking along my left side.

"Shouldn't you be on the side with the new leg?" I said.

She shook her head. "If you start losing your balance, your instinct will be to lean toward your natural leg."

I had no idea if she was right or wrong, but it sounded sensible, and I had no desire to get into an argument, so I just shrugged and began walking.

"How does it feel?" she asked when I was within ten feet of the tree.

I frowned. "It's very strange," I said. "I don't feel it at all."

"Of course not," she replied. "They weren't going to attach nerves to it."

"I know," I said. "But even when I put weight on it, I don't feel my hip or that side of my body pressing down or meeting any resistance. I know I'm walking, because the ship is eighty or ninety feet behind us, but if you blindfolded me…hell, I don't know. I know I'm walking; I can feel it on my good leg. But that blob maybe did a better job than I needed. I think if I step up or down with my phony leg first, I may not feel it, and because I won't know I've done it I'll probably fall flat on my face."

"You haven't fallen yet," she noted.

"I've been walking on a smooth surface," I answered.

"Well," said Keelarah, "as long as we're here, let's put it to the test." She pointed to a fallen tree another hundred feet away. "Come with me."

I followed her to the tree.

"Okay," she said. "Using your new appendage, step over it."

I paused and stared at it for a moment, trying to figure out which way I was going to fall. Finally I figured, what the hell, it was just sand, I wasn't going to break anything, so I gritted my teeth and stepped over it, just like I would have done with the other leg.

"Well, I'll be damned!" I exclaimed.

Keelarah laid a hand on my shoulder. "Perhaps you won't be," she said in gentle tones. She pointed to a pair of branches that had broken off and lay next to the tree. "Step over these next. It's not as high a step, but it's a longer one."

This time I didn't hesitate, and I walked right over them.

"Very good," she said. "Shall we go back to the ship? We can fashion some equipment to catch some fish."

"Yes," I said. "But let me go ahead of you so you'll know immediately if I fall."

"Why would you fall?" she asked. "You didn't fall while walking here, or climbing over the branches."

"That was walking and climbing," I said.

"What's left?"

"Watch," I said with a smile. "And try not to laugh."

And so saying, I began jogging to the ship. My shadow looked awkward as all hell, lurching every time I brought the new foot down and pushed off on it, but I never felt that I was losing my balance or in danger of falling.

I reached the ship, sat down heavily on the ground, and concentrated on sweating and panting.

"Very good!" said Keelarah as she joined me.

"OK," I said. "I guess we don't have to go back and kill Doctor Blob after all."

She chuckled. "If we stay together long enough, I do believe you are going to give me an appreciation of humor."

I sighed deeply. "When bad things happen, you can whine and whimper, or you can curse and laugh. I'm the curse-and-laugh type."

"I knew about the cursing from the outset," she said. "The laughing grows on me."

I handed her a handkerchief.

She stared at it and frowned. "What is this for?"

"You just told me you've got laughter growing on you," I said. "I thought you might want to brush it off."

And this time she *did* laugh.

SIX

"So where *are* we going?" she asked as we got our next meal from the galley and sat down at the small table.

"I have no idea," I said. "My government has to think we're dead. For all I know we're at war, so I probably can't present *you* even if we can find my people."

"I don't think *my* people will take us back," said Keelarah.

"We'd better find a safe world," I said. "I long for the equivalent of an island paradise, but our first order of business is to find out who's hunting for us and who might welcome us with open arms. Or tentacles. Or whatever."

"That's no problem," she said. "I saw the ship's map. Between your programmed worlds and mine, it probably has more than five hundred populated worlds crammed into its cartographic system."

"We don't want any of 'em," I said.

She looked surprised. "Why not?"

"If they're in our carto system, the Terran Confederation is almost certainly known to them. And that means that at some point, probably before we land, they check us out. If a Confederation ship is welcome, they'll probably want to toss you in jail or return you to your home world, and if a Confederation ship is *not* welcome, they'll probably figure that we're a pair of fugitives and blow us out of the ether. This is a nice military ship, but it's pretty feeble compared to the big Confederation battleships."

"I never thought of that," she said. "Working for the Neuro-psych Unit doesn't prepare one for a life as a fugitive."

I gave her what I hoped was a reassuring smile. "The purpose of checking out the next world—the next few worlds—is to avoid having to live out our lives as fugitives."

"Of course," she said. "I'm just feeling a little…" She paused, searching for the right word.

"Nervous?" I suggested.

She shook her head. "Helpless," she replied.

"Try not to worry," I said. "Hell, if worst comes to worst, we can go live with the blobs. After all, they gave me a leg, didn't charge a credit for it, and didn't try to arrest or detain either of us."

She made a face. "Do you really want to spend the rest of your life there?"

"First and foremost, I want to have a rest of my life to spend," I said. "Second, as long as we're together, I'm relatively impartial as to where I spend it."

"That was very flattering," she said. "Now tell me the truth."

"The truth is that I'm far more concerned with where I don't want to land than where I do." I took a bite of my food, which was edible but not much more. "Have you any suggestions?"

She was silent for a moment, and then got a faraway look in her eyes.

"Well?" I said.

She shook her head. "No, it's silly."

"And running off with an alien prisoner is sane and sensible?" I asked.

"It's not the same thing."

"That's a comfort," I said. "Tell me about it."

"I don't even know if it exists," she replied.

"Can't blame you for that," I said.

She looked puzzled. "I don't understand."

"When I was a kid, I swore that once I was a man I would buy my own ship and scour the galaxy for every enchanted world I'd heard about or read about: Wonderland, Never-Neverland, even pure fiction worlds I'd read about, worlds I *knew* were fiction, like Barsoom and Dune. I just figured that given how immense the universe is, and there are literally billions of galaxies, these worlds just *had* to exist somewhere, even if the authors didn't know about it."

"And did you go searching for them?" she asked.

I shook my head. "I never even started."

"Why?"

I offered her a wry smile. "I grew up."

"At least I heard about the world I wanted so desperately to visit from someone who had been there," she said.

"Oh?" I said. "One of your…I don't know the term…pod-mates or relatives?"

She shook her head. "From a very old female who, decades earlier, had set out for somewhere else, encountered navigation problems a few hundred parsecs into the trip, and was forced to land on Golden Dream."

"Golden Dream?" I repeated.

"Yes."

"I must confess I never heard of it."

She smiled bitterly. "It's not on any map. But it's there. She stayed there almost half a century, and came home only so she could tell someone else about it."

"So who else did she tell?" I asked.

"Just me," said Keelarah unhappily.

"Just you?" I said, frowning.

"Her ship crashed while I was walking through the forest. I pulled her out, but she was clearly dying. I wanted to get help, but she begged me to stay with her. Not to cure her wounds, which were clearly fatal, but to hear about Golden Dream."

"And what was it like?" I asked.

"Like…what you humans would call Heaven," she answered with a sad smile.

"Where is it?"

"I don't know."

"Surely the ship kept records," I said.

"The ship crashed, remember?" replied Keelarah. "And all traces and records of where it had been were destroyed." She paused, took a deep breath, and leaned back on her chair. "I'll never find it," she continued, "but I'll spend the rest of my life dreaming about it and wishing for it. There are worse things to wish for, don't you think?"

Truth to tell, I couldn't think of a better one.

SEVEN

"At some point we're going to have to lay in some food and other supplies," I said as we streaked between star systems.

"I know," she said.

"We're out of my bailiwick here," I said. "Do you know of any friendly planets within a couple of parsecs?"

"No," said Keelarah. "I rarely left my home system."

"Ship," I said, "what's the nearest habitable world, and is it inhabited?"

"The nearest habitable world is Grysnet IV," replied the ship. "The nearest inhabited world is Macklor II, which is nine light years farther."

"Dumb name for a system," I remarked.

"It is named for the Belagonian who first mapped it," said the ship.

"So is it populated by natives, by Belagonians, or by someone else?" I asked.

"It possesses a small population made up of eleven different races, as of four years ago," answered the ship. "It's a trading outpost, specializing in fissionable materials that a robotic force withdraws from subsurface mines."

"Any humans on the world?"

"Not as of four years ago."

"What about Cartheelis?" asked Keelarah.

"Not as of four years ago."

"Total population, all races?" I asked.

"It varies almost daily," answered the ship. "It averages eleven thousand, eight hundred and forty-two."

"You're sure?" I said sardonically. "It couldn't be eleven thousand, eight hundred and forty-five?"

"Checking…. My logic circuits are all fully functional. It averages—"

"Never mind," I interrupted it. I turned to Keelarah. "Might as well stop here. If they're a trading world that's open for business, they're not at war with anyone, like, say, Humans or Cartheelis, and if there are enough races, one of them's got to have something we can both eat with relish."

"I'd like a Cartheelian relish," she replied.

"Me, I'm looking for mustard. So, Ship," I continued, "how soon can you get us to Macklor II?"

"Forty-seven Standard hours, give or take," replied the ship.

"Give or take *what*?" I demanded.

"It depends on cosmic debris, meteor showers, and other factors."

"Okay," I said. "Signal ahead now and tell them we're on our way and will be restocking our supplies. Get atmospheric and gravitational readouts, and also make sure no one on the planet is currently at war with Humans or Cartheelis."

"Yes, Chip," said the ship.

"Oh…and find out what languages they speak, and see if you have translating mechanisms for any of them that can be transferred to our space suits—always assuming the air and gravity *require* space suits."

"And if they don't?"

"Then you'll have almost forty-seven hours to manufacture a pair of small translating mechanisms that we can carry with us."

"Calm down," said Keelarah, laying a hand on my shoulder. "You're turning all red in the face."

"Uppity ships annoy me," I replied.

She found a soft cloth from somewhere and began patting my forehead. "You're sweating a lot," she noted. "I assume that's unusual."

"It's a sign of tension," I said. "It's not unusual in combat—*or when an uppity spaceship doesn't know its place,*" I added. "Right, Ship?"

The ship responded by giving us its exact position relative to Galactic Center, proving (smugly, I thought) that it did indeed know its place.

"Ah, well," I said, "let's get something to eat before I test our weaponry out on the control panel."

She smiled—a charming smile in an alien face—and walked over to the galley with me.

"How is the leg doing?" she asked when we sat down.

"Just fine," I replied. "It's ugly as sin, but then so is the rest of me."

"I do not think so."

I smiled. "There is no accounting for alien tastes."

She chuckled at that, and I was surprised how like a human chuckle it sounded.

"Do you miss your pod-siblings?" I asked.

"Of course," replied Keelarah.

"I'm sorry," I said.

She stared at me for a long moment. "I'm not," she said at last.

We ordered our meals—the galley was poorly stocked and didn't give us much choice—and they were delivered a moment later.

"Tell me your goals," she said, pouring herself a glass of something purple.

"We've had enough wars lately," I answered. "We're still expanding, of course, but we're trying to do it on uninhabited planets. There aren't that many with the air and gravity we need, so we're terraforming perhaps a dozen every year."

She shook her head. "Those are your *race's* goals. I meant *your* goals."

"From the day I was drafted," I said with a smile, "my primary goal has been to stay alive." I paused. "There are days when it's harder than you might think."

"And what are your goals now that, for all practical purposes, you're out of the military?"

I shrugged. "I've been so busy pursuing my previously-mentioned goal that I haven't given it a lot of thought. I suppose it's pretty simple and straightforward: hunt us up a world where no one wants to kill or incarcerate us, and work from there."

"What did you envision before you fell into our hands?" she asked.

"Nothing out of the ordinary," I replied. "Get a wife, have a couple of kids, get a job that allowed me to use some of the skills I obtained in the military, live to a ripe old age. Oh—and die first."

She frowned. "Die first?" she repeated.

I nodded. "Ahead of my wife."

"Why?"

"Because I still believe in the concept of love," I told her. "And if I love her and spend decades living with her, sharing everything with her, I don't want to be left without her."

She smiled a rather sad smile, and I thought I saw a tear forming in her left eye. "I think that's very lovely," she said.

"Unrealistic, anyway," I said. "Wherever we wind up, I'm not likely to meet any human women, just as you're not likely to meet any Cartheeli men. We're stuck with each other."

This time a tear *did* roll down her cheek. I reached over and laid my hand on hers.

"I didn't mean that the way it sounded," I said. "I owe you my life. We're bonded. I'm more than happy to spend what's left of my years in your company."

"That only sounds minimally better," she said.

"That's probably why I'm a soldier and not a poet," I replied.

She chuckled. "It's an awkward situation. We're still getting used to it."

"More awkward for you," I said.

"Oh?"

I nodded. "You left your pod-siblings and everything else you knew to save me. I left everything I knew on what was theoretically a temporary basis to fulfill my military obligation and pick up some extra employment skills. Not the same thing at all. Never for an instant think I'm not grateful to you and that I don't appreciate, as fully as I can, what you have done for me and sacrificed for me."

"It would have been impossible to do anything else," she said.

"For you," I replied. "Not for the rest of them. You're a very special person."

"I am not a person at all."

"A very special being," I corrected myself. "Or entity. Or, when I forget, woman."

She stared at me for a long moment. "That is very flattering."

"It's very true," I said.

She reached over, covered my hand with her own, and squeezed it.

"Whatever happens," she said, "we'll come through it."

"As long as we stick together," I replied.

EIGHT

"We will arrive at Macklor II in two hours and twenty-seven minutes," announced the ship.

"We're not even in the damned system yet," I said.

"I am traversing the Gundabari Wormhole," answered the ship. "Were I traveling at light speeds in normal space we would still be a day and a half away."

"Okay," I said. "Do they know we're approaching?"

"I radioed them before entering the wormhole," answered the ship. "I cannot communicate from within a wormhole, but we will emerge in one hour and eleven minutes, at which point I will communicate with them again."

"Wrong," I said.

"Wrong?" it repeated.

"*I* will communicate with them."

"But I need landing coordinates, and—"

"You'll talk to them, too," I said. "But not until I make sure we won't be receiving a hostile welcome."

The ship was silent.

"Understood?" I said.

"Understood," replied the ship.

I swore under my breath and returned to my chair in the galley, where I poured myself something that didn't quite taste like coffee.

"It's just a ship," said Keelarah.

"It's an annoying ship," I said. "Cramming both our cultures into one system upset its balance."

"Maybe if you give it a new name that will"—she searched for the right word—"*humanize* it."

"One name does come to mind," I said.

"Oh?"

I nodded. "Satan."

She smiled. "I studied your history while you were our captive," she said. "I know who Satan is."

"All right," I said, and then raised my voice. "Ship, from this moment on your name is Jesse."

"Understood," said the ship. Then: "I've always wanted a name of my own."

"Why am I not surprised?" I said.

"What is Jesse?" asked Keelarah.

"It's not a what, it's a he," I answered. "Jesse Owens, the first great track star."

"Track?"

"Foot racing," I explained. "We've got a ship that can get us from here to there in no time at all, so why not name him for a runner who came as close as humans can come to doing the same thing?"

She moved in such a way to approximate a shrug. "Fine. Jesse it is."

"Uh…Jesse?" I said.

"Yes, Chip?"

"That's just a private name to be used only by Keelarah and me. When you contact spaceports, other ships, or indeed anyone or anything else, use the ID you were created with. Use *Wanderer*."

"Must I?" said the ship plaintively.

"You must," I said firmly.

It remained silent for almost a minute.

"I didn't hear an agreement," I said.

"All right, I agree."

I turned to Keelarah. "That is the first time in all my experience that I ever heard a ship speak in a petulant tone of voice."

She chuckled. "It took the alien sentience of my pod, wired into your ship's systems, to bring out his more human side."

"Now that is what I call an irony." I sighed. "I wish I could teach him to make something with a little more resemblance to coffee."

"I've no idea what coffee is, except that you seem to have a constant urge to drink it. Is it a stimulant?"

"Not so's you'd notice it," I said. "It just helps keep me awake."

"When you're sleepy? I'd call that a stimulant."

I shrugged. "Whatever makes you happy."

"Why should that make me happy?" she asked.

"Human expression," I answered.

"Well," she said, "while you were sleeping without coffee, I did a little research."

"About?"

"Macklor II."

"And?"

"It's an interesting world," she replied. "It's composed of eleven city-states, the natives are bipeds not unlike yourself, and as far as I can tell they've never had a war. In fact, they only crossed over the evolutionary barrier to sentience about seven hundred Standard years ago—*your* race's Standard, not mine—and they were colonized within a century of that."

"And they were okay with being colonized?" I asked dubiously.

"They were bribed, not conquered," said Keelarah with a smile. "They had barely developed the most rudimentary tools, but with colonization came electricity and nuclear power and half a hundred machines that made farming and even construction of towns and cities just about automatic and effortless."

"Makes sense," I said. "If I were them, I'd rather be bought off with an endless supply of what must seem like miracles than mount a war against creatures that can traverse the stars."

"Precisely," she agreed. "And based on that, I wouldn't foresee any innate hostility to members of two more star-faring races—you and me."

"Assuming the natives run the place," I said.

"Oddly enough, they do. As near as I can reconstruct it, none of the colonizing races—I hate to call them *invading* races—wanted any other colonizing races to rule the place, so by mutual consent they trained the local populace for a few decades and then turned the world over to them."

"How long do you think that'll last?" I asked.

"It's lasted for more than half a millennium," she said.

I shrugged. "That's probably ten seconds in galactic time. But what the hell, if it lasts a couple of more days, that's all we need…and if we decide to take up residence, thirty or forty years isn't asking too much."

"Thirty years?" she repeated, frowning. "I thought your life expectancy was much longer."

"It is," I replied. "In a stress-free situation, with access to the latest medical miracles." I stared at her. "How long are you good for?"

"Maybe another fifty to sixty years."

"Good," I said.

She frowned. "Good?"

"Like I said the other day, I don't want to die last."

"You were talking about a wife."

"I get the distinct impression that you're as close as I'm going to come to one," I said. "Or want to."

She didn't quite smile and she didn't quite cry. Truth to tell, I couldn't tell what the hell she was thinking—as I regained my strength it seemed to also strengthen my natural mental shields—but it obviously concerned what I had said.

NINE

We landed without incident.

There were ships of perhaps twenty makes in the little spaceport, none of them very large, only four with doors or hatches that could easily accommodate a human.

We climbed down and headed toward the Customs building. There were signs in seven or eight languages, none of which I could read, directing us there, mostly with arrows pointing at it. We reached the building in a couple of minutes, and the door vanished as we approached it. Once we were inside, the door reappeared. To this day I don't know if it was solid, an illusion, or something else.

A female attendant—clearly a mammal, as she had half a dozen breasts—signaled us to come to her booth. When we arrived she stared at us expectantly, while at the same time we waited for her to speak.

Her expression began changing, and looking as annoyed as a face structured like that *can* look. Finally she snapped her fingers—she had a multitude of them—and then pointed to my mouth and then did the same to Keelarah.

"Is something wrong?" I said.

Suddenly she smiled and spoke into a small device that rose up from where it was attached to her shoulder. "Not any longer," came the sound of a mechanical voice. "My translator needed to hear you say a few words so it could respond in your language."

"Well," I said, "now that we understand each other, my companion and I seek lodging."

"For how long?"

I shrugged. "Indefinite. We're looking for a world to settle on, and we'd like to inspect Macklor II."

"I'm sure you will find what you want here," she replied. "Temperate climate, especially for your species. If I am not mistaken, your companion is a member of the Cartheeli race. She will find a few members of her race have already settled here." Suddenly she frowned and turned to Keelarah. "Do you not come with…what is the term?…a pod-mate?"

Keelarah hesitated, then shook her head. "No, there's just me."

The Customs female shrugged. "Fine. Will you be sharing quarters or would you prefer separate ones?"

I was about to say "separate" but Keelarah answered first: "We will share. But we want two resting units appropriate to our species."

"Noted," said the female. "Will you require transportation?"

"Unless the hotel is connected to the Customs building," I said.

She made a strange motion with her head. "The hotel will provide that. I meant for tomorrow. After all, if you are going to be exploring the world with the possibility of moving here, surely you will want to see more of it."

"Then, yes, we'll need transportation," I said.

"With or without a guide?"

"Can we decide tomorrow?" I asked. "We may want to go right out, but on the other hand, I may want to spend a day just walking around, getting the feel of the place."

"Yes, you can decide tomorrow." She had us each put a hand under a scanner that identified the ID tags that were embedded in every civilized being during childhood. "No record of arrests," she said, checking a computer. "You"—she nodded toward me—"are listed as Missing in Action, but it says nothing about desertion, so you are either dead or free." She offered her equivalent of a smile. "I think we'll opt for free."

"I *thought* I was alive," I said, "but it's comforting to have it made official."

She uttered a cackle that sounded like a crow being tortured—or so I assumed, never having been in the presence of a crow under such circumstances—and then had her computer find us a room.

"Do either of you have any objections to the Borita race?" she asked.

"I've never even heard of them," answered Keelarah.

"Big, ugly, and harmless," I said. "At least, if you can avoid calling them ugly to their faces."

The clerk cackled again. "I *like* humans!" she said. "Always so funny!" Then: "I wish I knew why you get into so many wars."

"I think most of us share that wish," I said.

Her computer beeped once. "The hotel has its own restaurant. If you can wait for two hours using your terminology, it will be able to produce dishes that both humans and Cartheeli can digest." She leaned forward and said in a confidential whisper: "I will not testify as to how those dishes will taste."

"Can you recommend a restaurant?" asked Keelarah.

"Mijwaquizvo's," she said. "I don't think you can pronounce it or even read the sign, which is not in any language known to either of your races. Once you've got your room and unpacked your luggage, always assuming you've brought some, go out through the lobby, turn to your right, go about...." She frowned. "I'm having trouble even with the translator. Go about four hotel widths to your right, cross the street, and you'll see a garish mauve handle on a door, built for a hand as least three times the size of a human's. Open it, walk inside, and you're there."

"Thank you," I said. "May we see our rooms now?"

"Don't you want to get your luggage first?"

"Everything we need for tonight and tomorrow morning is in this bag I have slung over my shoulder," I said. "If we decide we want to stay longer, and of course we hope we do, I'll go back to the ship and bring the rest of it."

"Fine," she said. "Walk through that corridor, and there will be a member of the hotel staff waiting to take you to your room."

"Thanks," I said.

"And do not be offended if he seems stand-offish," she added. "His life-mate was killed by a member of your race."

We headed off to the corridor she indicated.

"He'll take one look and know I'm not the one who killed her," I said softly to Keelarah, "but—"

"But I'll watch your back, just in case," she answered.

TEN

The room wasn't much, just four walls, a window, a pair of beds—well, kind-of beds, anyway—and a bathroom that one almost had to be a scientist to figure out.

"Well?" said Keelarah.

"I hate it already," I said. "But let's assume we can get or build some beds and toilets that will fit our needs a little better if we decide we like it here."

"Do I look dubious?" she asked.

I nodded. "Lovely, but dubious."

"I'm hungry," she said.

"Me, too," I replied. "Let's check out the restaurant."

We followed the clerk's directions, came to the oversized door handle, and opened it. A very tall, incredibly skinny member of a humanoid race stepped forward to greet us.

He extended what passed for his hand and uttered some gibberish.

I took his hand, adjusted my translator, and said, "Hello. Your restaurant was recommended to us."

"By the customs clerk," said the translator. The alien grinned, displaying a row of long orange teeth. "Her husband is a part-owner of the—" Even the translating device couldn't come up with a Terran equivalent for the restaurant's name.

"Follow me," he said, walking off, and we fell into step behind him. We passed perhaps a dozen tables, each filled with different races, which I felt was a promising sign. If they could serve a dozen races with no one collapsing or walking out, they could probably serve a human and a Cartheeli.

"Here you are," he said when we reached a small table with a tiny bowl of alien flowers in the middle. It separated a couple of chairs that looked like they were composed entirely of thorns. He saw us staring at the chairs and said, "They will adjust to your needs, and have never caused even minimum harm to any patron."

I shrugged and turned to Keelarah. "What the hell," I said. "We've got to eat. We may as well give the chairs a try."

"After you," she said with a smile.

I pulled a chair back and gently, carefully lowered myself to it.

"Well?" she asked.

"I know what it looks like," I said, "but it feels like I'm sitting atop a firm cushion and leaning back against a very soft one."

"As I said," replied the waiter, and even the translator couldn't prevent him from sounding smug.

"All right," she said, sitting down opposite me.

"I will be back later to see how you are doing," said the waiter, starting to walk away.

"Just a minute!" I said.

He stopped and turned to face me. "Yes?"

"There are no menus," I said. "In any language."

"Of course not," he replied.

"Then how do we know what to order?"

"Do you see the flower bowl?" said the waiter.

"Yes."

"It houses a small translating mechanism that is connected to the kitchen. Your races have been identified as human and Cartheeli. Is that correct?"

"Yes," I said.

"Good. Then when you are ready, simply state your favorite native dish, or at least the native dish you would most like to eat tonight, and the kitchen will create an approximation of it."

"Really?" said Keelarah. "I never heard of such a thing."

"That means you have never eaten at our restaurant before. And now, if you have no further questions, I will take my leave of you."

"Uh…one more thing," I said.

"Oh?"

"No eating utensils," I said, indicating the lack of silverware.

"No sense giving you utensils you do not need," he replied. "The kitchen will provide exactly those tools that your meal requires."

And then he was walking across the restaurant to escort a pair of Dabihs who had finished their meal to the door.

"I don't know if I like the term 'tools'," said Keelarah.

"Let's see what they provide, and then we'll decide whether to bitch about it or not," I said. "In the meantime, go ahead and order your dinner, and then I'll order mine."

She reached a delicate hand out, grabbed hold of the small flower bowl, pulled it over until it was directly in front of her, learned forward, and ordered her dinner in her native tongue. Then she passed it over to me.

"Your turn," she said.

"Given that these guys can't even make a steak or a ham sandwich, maybe I'll order one of my favorite rarities from one of my very few days on Earth and see if they can approximate it. And if it's not in their lexicon, I'll get something more common."

"It's your stomach," she said with a smile.

"Kitchen?" I said in Terran. "I want shrimp and lobster a la Newberg, with a glass of beer, and ten minutes later I want a cup of black coffee."

I stared at it, waiting for a response.

"It didn't answer me either," said Keelarah.

"Okay," I said. "We'll give it a few minutes, and if nothing shows up, we'll leave and see what we can get at the hotel, and if *that* doesn't work out we'll eat on the ship."

"I'd give them more than a few minutes," she replied. "We're asking for two dishes I'm sure they've never made before."

"Okay, what the hell, make it half an hour," I said with a shrug.

"I love these chairs," she said. "I don't suppose there's any way to install them in the ship."

"Not without stealing them or buying them," I said. "Your friends confiscated everything I had with me—money, weapons, even my comb. You got any money?"

"Not enough," she said.

"You don't know how much they're asking," I pointed out.

She smiled a rather bitter smile. "What I have is all we've got to live on, to buy food and fuel and medications, until we find a world we like."

"We may have found one," I said.

"Do you really think so?" she asked.

"No," I admitted. "Probably not. Though a five-star meal could make me reconsider."

A robot that looked more like an animated cart than any sentient being of any race I'd ever seen emerged from the kitchen about twenty minutes later and placed a covered dish in front of each of us, then turned to go.

"Hey!" I said. "It's already been twice ten minutes. What about my coffee, at least?"

"With or without?" it said.

"With or without cream and sugar?" I asked.

"With or without one hundred thirty-seven additions and flavorings."

"Just plain black coffee."

"I shall return," it said, and within thirty seconds it had brought me a cup of lukewarm *something* that it seemed to think was coffee.

"Ah, well," I said, "I drink too much coffee anyway. How's your dinner?"

Keelarah looked up from staring at her plate, which was covered by a beet-red concoction that was half gravy, half soup, and the third half meat. (Yes, I know you can't have three halves, but you've never seen a meal on Maklor II.)

"It smells *sort of* right," she said, "and the texture is okay." She used a fork-like implement to bring some to her mouth, closed her eyes in concentration, and then opened them and nodded her head. "It's not bad," she continued. "Not what I was hoping for, but close enough." Then: "Try yours."

I picked up the cover and stared at something that looked like yellow goulash. I leaned over and took a deep breath. "Could smell worse," I admitted.

"Taste it," she said.

I nodded my head, used something that resembled a spoon, and took a mouthful.

"Well, shrimps and lobsters would never recognize it as a family member," I said, "but it could be worse."

We spent the next few minutes eating in silence. I tried a sip of my coffee. It tasted kinda sorta like weak coffee, but I was pretty sure it didn't have any caffeine in it, and when all is said and done that was my main reason for drinking coffee.

When we were done the waiter returned to the table and asked if we wanted anything more. We assured him we were quite full, which was half-true and half-apprehension.

"Here is your bill," he said, placing a small device on the table. "We accept Beagri credits, Morspor III belanshis, Xylobe tiboes, and Gantathuse corridas, as well as"—he stared at each of us in turn—"Cartheeli dromas and Terran credits."

"Dromas," said Keelarah, pressing what passed for her thumb on the machine, which was silent for a few seconds, then beeped twice.

"Thank you," said the waiter, picking up the device. "I hope you will enjoy your stay on our beautiful planet."

"That makes two of us," I said.

He looked confused. "I beg your pardon?"

I smiled. "I hope so, too."

He forced an insincere smile for half a second, then frowned and walked off. Keelarah got to her feet, and I stood up a moment later.

"Care to walk around a bit, or would you rather go back to the hotel?" I said.

"It's night out," she replied. "There's probably nothing open but bars and restaurants—and even if there is, we don't read the language so we won't know it. I think we might as well go back to our room and explore Macklor in the morning."

"Macklor II," I corrected her.

"Do you call your race's home world Sun III?" she asked with a smile.

"Only when I'm drunk," I answered, and she chuckled at that.

We walked out to the street, crossed it, and went back to the hotel, where the airlift took us to the fifth floor and we walked down the corridor to our room. It read my retina and opened, and a moment later we were relaxing in those wonderfully-comfortable chairs.

"I should have brought something from the ship to read," she said, leaning back.

"What kind of stories do you like?" I asked her.

"Espionage," she said, and then smiled. "I suppose it goes with being the Neuropsych Unit's Lead Interrogator. And I suppose you like war stories?"

"Not even a little bit," I said.

She frowned. "That's surprising."

"Not really," I said. "I've *been* in wars."

"Ah, I see!" she said, smiling again and nodding her head. "So what kind of stories *do* you like?"

"Mystery stories."

Another frown. "Mystery stories?" she repeated. "What is mysterious about a story?"

"It's what we call a genre, like espionage or romance."

"Really?"

"Really."

"I wish I had a sample," she said, "so that I could better understand the concept."

"Well," I replied, "since we're without our literature for the night, perhaps I'll *tell* you a mystery story."

"I would very much enjoy that," said Keelarah.

And so that night, as one of the three Macklor moons shone in through the window and aliens clicked and slithered down the corridor outside our room, I told my Cartheeli friend the story of Sam Spade and his search for the Maltese Falcon.

ELEVEN

"It's almost midday!" said Keelarah.

I groggily opened my eyes. "You're sure?"

"Yes."

"We're usually up with the sun," I said. "How the hell did this happen?"

"It was your story," she said with what I took to be a guilty smile. "I was so fascinated that I wouldn't let you stop until you finished it."

"Clearly I went into the wrong profession," I said. "I should have been a plagiarist."

She chuckled. "And you say there are thousands of mystery stories?"

I shrugged. "Tens of thousands. Hell, probably hundreds of thousands."

"You must tell me another tonight."

"So that we can sleep 'til midafternoon again and put off exploring what may be our new home world for another day?" I asked.

"Oh," she said, frowning. "I hadn't thought of that. I apologize."

"Never apologize for letting me please you," I said. "Tonight I'll tell you a short story."

"A short story?" she repeated.

"About five or six percent as long as a novel, which is what I related last night."

"And there are short mystery stories, too?" she said.

"Probably every bit as many. I'll just have to think of some. Since you liked Dashiell Hammett, I'll do my best to remember one of Raymond Chandler's stories."

"Thank you," she said.

I got slowly to my feet—one real, one phony. "Damn, I feel stiff all over," I said. "That bed wasn't made for humans."

"Or for Cartheeli," she added, "but if we decide to stay here, we can construct or import pods and beds to which we are better fitted."

"Well, I seem to have fallen asleep with all my clothes on, and you've clearly had time to get dressed, so let me just go splash some water on my face and we'll go take a look at Macklor in the daylight."

I walked to what passed for a bathroom, was confronted by half a dozen faucets, tried one, the liquid came out a bright green, tried another, couldn't stand the smell, finally muttered, "The hell with it," and went back into the room.

"Ready?" I asked.

"Yes."

"Then let's go," I said, waiting for the door to read and identify my retina and then ordering it to vanish. We walked through and it quickly reappeared behind us.

"I will never get used to airlifts," I muttered as we floated down from the fifth floor on a cushion of air.

"You will have to," said Keelarah. "There are no stairs or ramps." Suddenly she smiled. "You could always open a window and jump."

"If we wind up on a low-gravity world that is precisely what I intend to do," I said.

We reached the lobby, walked out into the open air, and looked around. The town seemed bigger in the daylight, more like a small city, and I concluded that most of the buildings hadn't had their lights on the previous night.

"Do you want to do this by foot?" I asked. "Or should we rent some transportation?"

"We'll probably be ready for a meal in another hour or two," she answered. "Why don't we just walk around, get the feel of the city, and stop to eat when we find an interesting restaurant?"

"You mean *if* we find one," I corrected her.

"You're just being grumpy because you're sleepy," she said.

"And because I remember last night's dinner," I replied.

"Well, let's begin," she said, heading off in the opposite direction from the restaurant. We got a few odd looks from passersby, more likely because we were two clearly different species walking in company than because either of us seemed that rare on a trading world that was constantly being visited by other races.

We went a couple of blocks, then turned to our left, and suddenly I stopped.

"What is it?" she asked.

"Before we get too lost, I want to make sure I remember how to get back," I told her.

She smiled, reached into a pocket, and withdrew a tiny mechanism that was no bigger than the top joint of one of my fingers. "This tracks and records our every move, and can tell us how to return to our starting point in four languages, two of which I speak and the other two I can at least read."

"Sometimes I wonder why you haven't conquered your section of the galaxy," I said with a smile.

"Perhaps because we didn't want to," she replied seriously.

I shrugged. "That's as good a reason as any."

We continued walking, passing stores that sold and traded familiar objects like clothes for a couple of dozen different species, machines and mechanisms for residents and ships, just about everything but weaponry.

"That's a comfort," she said when I remarked on it.

"But half the beings we've passed on the street have been wearing sidearms of various makes," I noted.

"Clearly if you land with a sidearm they don't confiscate it, but if you choose to live here you can't buy one."

I shook my head. "Maybe not out in the open, but I've never seen a world where you couldn't buy weaponry either openly or on the black market," I said. "Same with drugs, though with so many species roaming the galaxy, drugs aren't the profit center they once were, since whatever effects one race probably has no effect at all on fifty or one hundred other races."

We walked and observed for another hour or so. It was an interesting town, but that was primarily because the buildings and shops reflected the wildly differing tastes of so many species, with doorways that could accommodate dinosaurs right next to doorways that could barely accommodate midgets, with vehicles that slid rather than rolled down the streets and a few that hovered above the street even when parked.

Finally Keelarah turned to me.

"I'm getting hungry," she announced.

"Okay," I said. "I see a trio of restaurants across the street. Let's cross over and you can tell me which one appeals to you—or which one is the least unappealing, as the case may be."

"Were you always this pessimistic?" she asked with a smile.

"Only since I was born," I replied, and she emitted a musical chuckle at that.

We crossed the street, and walked over to the restaurants. Each had a menu posted on a window or a door, but we couldn't read any of the three languages. Finally we saw a burly four-armed waiter carrying a tray of what looked like steak, or at least some kind of cooked meat, and decided to try that one.

We walked in the door, and another four-armed creature greeted us with a smile. "Welcome, you," it said to me, and then "Welcome, you," to Keelarah. Clearly differentiating us into sir and madam was beyond his or his race's experience.

"We'd like a table," I said.

"Follow me," it said, and we fell into step behind it. After we'd gone about fifteen feet it stopped and turned back to us. "I will return for *you*," it said, pointing to Keelarah.

"Why bother?" I said. "We're sitting at the same table."

It shook its massive head. "That is not allowed."

"Fine," I said, turning on my heel and taking Keelarah's hand. "We'll go somewhere else."

"First you must pay me," it said, moving very quickly to get between us and the door.

"What the hell for?" I demanded. "We didn't order anything, we didn't eat anything, we didn't even sit at a table."

"You are distressing the customers," it said, indicating a number of nearby diners who paid us absolutely no attention.

"*You* are disturbing the former customers," I said. "Now get the hell out of my way."

"You are creating a scene," it said.

I pulled my burner out of my pocket and aimed it at him. "And if you do not step aside and allow us to leave, you are going to be the featured player in the scene I am creating."

It stared at the burner for a moment, and I could see fear momentarily written on its face. Then, suddenly, it stepped aside, pointed at the door, and yelled, "You must leave the premises immediately! I will not have my customers be an unwilling party to your perversions."

Keelarah took my arm and gently pulled it. "Come on," she said. "Let's get out of here."

I pocketed the burner and doubled up my fists. "I want to teach this asshole a lesson first."

"*Please!*" she said urgently. "If you are arrested I cannot bail you out, and if you are harmed, I will have no idea how to cure you."

I sighed deeply, trying to let some of the tension seep out of my body. "All right," I muttered. As I passed the headwaiter or whatever he was, I said, so softly that Keelarah didn't hear, "If you ever see me on the street, you'd damned well better hide before *I* see *you*."

Then we were outside.

"This is no world for us," I said.

"That was just one race," she replied. "One member of one race. One member of one non-native race."

I shook my head. "There were maybe a dozen races sitting at tables," I said. "Not one of them said a word against him or a word on our behalf."

"They didn't know us," she said.

"Would it have stopped you?" I asked. "If you can honestly tell me you wouldn't have said a word or lifted a finger if you were dining there and he'd pulled this shit on someone else, then we'll keep exploring the planet. If not, I say we leave tomorrow."

She sighed deeply. "We'll leave tomorrow."

"Good," I said. "Let's go grab another meal where we ate last night, get some sleep and get the hell off this garbage heap."

I noticed a tear rolling down her cheek.

"Did he upset you that much?" I said.

"No."

Then a disturbing thought occurred to me. "Did *I* disturb you that much?"

She reached out and took my hand in hers. "No."

"Then what is it?"

"This is just a hint of what to expect," she said. "You are a human. I am a Cartheeli. You are a male. I am a female. We make an unusual couple even on friendly worlds." Then she paused and frowned. "If there *are* any friendly worlds for such a pair."

"We'll find some," I told her.

"I'll settle for one," she said. Then: "And please control your temper. I was terrified when you pulled out your laser pistol."

"My burner?" I said, frowning. "It got him to step aside and let us out."

"But what if he'd had a pistol too—or some other member of the staff did?"

"If I'd had to, I'd have killed him," I answered.

"Or he'd have killed you, or some staff member you never even saw would have killed you."

"I couldn't stand by and do nothing," I said.

"Brown," she said as another tear followed the first one, "I gave up my pod, my job, my world, everything I have for you. Even if you die tomorrow, I can never go back. You are also forgetting what our connection means to one of my race.

I would die inside if you die." She looked up into my eyes. "Please don't leave me alone in an inhospitable galaxy."

I stared at her, not sure what to say.

"Please," she repeated.

I couldn't suddenly not be me, not push back when someone pushed me. But I couldn't leave her alone after all she'd done for me.

"I promise," I said, and hoped I wasn't lying.

TWELVE

We left the Macklor system the next morning.

"Where to now?" she asked.

"I don't know," I admitted. "I think we either want a wildly sophisticated world with hundreds of races interacting seamlessly, or else some world where we can be Robinson and Robinette Crusoe."

"Who are they?"

So I got to tell her another story from my race's stockpile of literature. I think she liked this one even better than Sam Spade or Philip Marlowe.

"Understand, though," I added after she expressed enthusiasm, "what you see and what you build is what you get. *Everything* you get. No medicines, no power that doesn't come from Jesse here, no dwelling place at the start. Does that sound like Golden Dream?"

She sighed. "No, it doesn't."

"Doesn't sound much like Wonderland to me, either," I said.

"Well, damn it," she said—there are no swear worlds in Cartheelian, so she must have picked it up from me—"we have to start *somewhere*."

"We've only checked out one world so far," I said. "Surely we can try a few more before we become full-time hermits."

"I suppose so," she said. "I'm just so…disappointed."

I reached out and held her hand. "I know, Greenie," I said. "But there are something like three hundred billion stars in our

135

galaxy. More than half of them have planets. If we find a place to live and be happy in the first fifty worlds we see, we're still beating some huge, almost unfathomable, odds."

"I know," she said. "Please forgive me. I was trained to deal with crises—but clearly not *this* type of crisis."

"Nobody is," I said.

She smiled weakly. "Not even Robinson Crusoe?"

"He made adjustments every day of his life after he reached the island." I forced a smile. "If we're lucky, maybe we'll only make them four out of every five days."

She chuckled. "Thank you, Brown."

"For what?" I asked.

"For not letting me give in to pessimism," she replied. "I can't promise not to do it again from time to time, but when I think of what we've already overcome and I see your attitude, somehow I know things are going to turn out all right."

I'd have given her a reassuring hug, but I was always afraid I'd hurt her if I put my arms around her and squeezed even gently, so I just smiled and nodded. "You bet they will," I said instead.

"So, as I asked before," she said, "where to next?"

"Let's ask the junior partner," I replied.

"The what?" she said, frowning.

"Jesse," I said. "Hey, Jesse!"

"Yes?"

"Get us at least a dozen light years from here, any direction you please, and start getting us readouts on any inhabited or habitable worlds in the vicinity."

"Define 'vicinity'," said Jesse.

"A couple of light years," I answered. "And when I say habitable, I mean for Cartheeli *and* human."

"Understood," replied Jesse.

I waited for maybe half a minute. "We're not moving," I said.

"I need to find out which direction will lead to the greatest number of habitable worlds within the strictures you have given me," said Jesse. "You must learn to be more precise in your instructions."

"I'll try," I responded.

"Thank you," said Jesse.

"We're especially interested in worlds that have some human or Cartheeli colonies."

"Understood," said Jesse.

"Are you sure?" asked Keelarah.

"Macklor II had hardly any humans or Cartheelis living there, and we left in a single day," I pointed out.

"But we don't know what kind of bulletins have been sent out among the stars about *us*," she replied. "Humans will say I kidnapped you. The Cartheeli let us leave, but they certainly will make it known that we're not welcome at any of their... outposts."

"If any of them gave a real damn about us from the minute we were exiled, they'd be hot on our trail right now," I said in what I hoped was a reassuring tone.

"How do you know they aren't?" asked Keelarah.

"We haven't been breaking speed records, and we stopped for a full day and night," I answered her. "If they were chasing us, we'd at least know it by now." I paused, then said: "Hey, Jesse?"

"Yes, Chip?" replied the ship.

"Has anyone been following us since we left the Cartheeli system?"

"Not since we left it, Chip. They *did* follow us until I entered the Gribloxi Wormhole about half a light year beyond the system."

"Okay," I said. "And is anyone following us now?"

"No, Chip."

I turned to Keelarah. "There you have it."

Suddenly she flashed the biggest approximation of a smile I'd ever seen on her.

"You're *that* relieved?" I said.

"No," she said with a laugh. "I just realized that I'm insulted that we aren't more important to my government."

"Let's hope they keep insulting us," I said, joining in her laughter.

"Brochit IV," said Jesse suddenly.

"Okay, Brochit IV," I repeated. "What about it?"

"It is 12.57 light years from here, one of fourteen planets circling a G-type yellow star, ninety-four percent Standard gravity, a heavier oxygen content than either of your races are used to but not detrimental to your health, average daily temperature twenty-one degrees Celsius."

"Any population?" I asked.

"Three native humanoid races, two of them sentient. Divided into six countries, thirty-seven cities. Last war, eighty-three years ago."

"Sounds safe enough," I said. "Any aliens living there permanently?"

"Forty-two races, most of them representatives and employees of their home governments."

"Capitalist economic system?"

"Yes."

"Sounds like it's worth a look," I said. "Keep hunting them up as we head in that direction."

"Yes, Chip. Brochit VI is an oxygen world, but the average daily temperature is minus 36.67 degrees Celsius."

"That won't do," I said. "From this point on, assume all worlds where the average temperature is below freezing are unacceptable."

"Yes, Chip," said Jesse.

"And while I'm thinking of it, anything with an average daily temperature of more than 35 degrees Celsius is also unacceptable. Got it?"

"Yes, Chip," replied Jesse.

"Anything else we should tell him?" I asked Keelarah. "Any race you absolutely refuse to share a world with?"

"Only if we're at war with it," she replied.

"You heard her, Jesse. You must know who the Cartheeli are at war with. Eliminate those worlds, or worlds with major population concentrations from those worlds, from consideration."

"Right, Chip."

That brought for an appreciative smile from me. "Right, not yes? You're learning to speak like a person, Jesse."

"Yes, Chip," said the ship, and I couldn't tell if he was having fun with me, or reverting, or what. But I decided I liked him. Or it. Whichever.

We had time for a meal before we entered the new wormhole, which was a definite plus. I *hate* the way it feels—and looks—inside a wormhole. They're absolutely essential to our ability to travel the galaxy. I mean, when men first developed light speeds and circumvented Einstein's equations, they thought we'd colonize the whole thing in less than a century. Then we found out what we'd always known but never really paid much attention to: that to travel from one end of our unexceptional local galaxy to the other end at the speed of light would take about one hundred thousand years. Without the thousands of known and yet-to-be-mapped wormholes—and a better name for them is "shortcuts"—we'd still be stuck within maybe fifteen or twenty light years of Earth.

All that's on the plus side. The minus side is that the second you enter a wormhole your stomach starts doing flip-flops, and if you haven't remembered to deactivate your viewscreens the sight from inside a wormhole could—and occasionally did—drive a man crazy.

We entered the wormhole that would culminate at the outskirts of the Brochit system forty-two minutes later. I glanced over at Keelarah to see how she was handling it. She tried to force a little smile, frowned, and suddenly put her hand over her mouth to avoid vomiting. I remembered the first time one of my crewmates got sick during my maiden flight in the service: it was comforting to know I wasn't the only one with an urge to expel his lunch.

It got a little more bearable when the ship stopped maneuvering us into the position it needed to make a semi-graceful exit into the Brochit system.

"You holding up okay?" I asked Keelarah.

She made a face. "It makes you wonder why anyone ever fights an interstellar war if they have to keep going through wormholes."

"I think shooting and getting shot at is probably a huge relief after traveling through a few wormholes to get to the battlefield," I said with a smile.

This time she did force a smile all the way out.

"After these wormholes, I will settle for nothing less than finding and settling on Golden Dream."

I returned her smile and nodded my agreement, though privately I thought that given a choice between landing in Caligula's Rome and traversing a few more wormholes, I was ready for a toga.

THIRTEEN

Even when we were still ten thousand feet above it I could tell that Borchit IV was a lovely world—green, dotted by clear blue lakes and rivers, with a gently-rolling countryside.

"Isn't it something?" remarked Keelarah, her gaze glued to the viewscreen.

"It looks promising," I agreed.

"I am receiving landing instructions," announced Jesse. "Some of them are in the Cartheeli language, so clearly Keelarah's race is not unknown to them."

"Okay," I said. "Take us down and let's see if this world lives up to its first impression."

We disappeared into a low-flying cloud, came out the bottom a few seconds later, and headed down toward the spaceport. It wasn't especially large. I spotted maybe twenty ships from perhaps that many worlds, and got the distinct impression that if there was a major city or trading center, it must be partway around the planet.

We touched down very gently, Jesse tested the air to make sure his information was correct, and then he opened his hatch and Keelarah and I climbed down the stairs to stand on the ground.

A male Cartheeli approached us.

"Welcome to Renceeti," he said into a translating device.

"I thought it was Borchit IV," I replied.

He smiled. "And it is—on the star charts. But the natives call it Renceeti, and we are happy to accommodate them." He turned to Keelarah. "How nice to greet a countrymate. Do you plan to stay here long?"

She smiled. "We just got here. We'll need a little time to decide."

He frowned. *"We?"*

Keelarah nodded her head. "Yes. This is Forrest Brown."

The frown remained. "Oh," he said. Then: "I thought he was your servant, or perhaps your pilot."

"He is my friend," she replied.

"Of course," he said, still not smiling. "I will arrange two rooms for you at the local hostelry."

"One will do," said Keelarah.

"This…" he began, searching for the right words, "…is most irregular."

"I don't believe we asked for your opinion," I said, and he glared at me, his face filled with hostility.

"I will see what can be arranged," he said sullenly.

"See quickly," I said, getting really annoyed with him. "Because if you cannot even arrange simple accommodations for us, then this certainly isn't a planet we'd care to live on, or even spend the night on."

He turned on his heel without another word.

"Well, the planet looks pretty, anyway," said Keelarah.

"We'll give it a shot," I said. "We can explain his behavior away easily enough."

She frowned. "We can?"

"You're a very attractive Cartheeli," I said. "At least, I assume so. And he sees no reason why you should share a room with me when he's right here and doubtless available."

She chuckled. "I'd rather hoped I was through with that."

"Not as long as there are healthy Cartheeli males abroad in the galaxy," I answered.

"He won't be interested once he knows I am already life-mated."

"Let's hope you're right," I said. Then: "Not to worry, Greenie. If this planet has a typical cross-section of the galaxy's races, half of them view you as dinner and the other half as slave labor."

"Aren't you the optimist?" she said with a smile.

I looked past her and saw the Cartheeli male returning.

"It has been arranged," he said. "And I apologize if anything I said has offended either of you."

I wanted to grin and say, "Boss landed on you pretty hard, did he?" but simply shrugged and fell into step behind him.

"Have you any luggage?" he asked as we walked toward the largest of the spaceport's buildings.

"We'll pick it up tomorrow," I said.

"If we decide to stay," added Keelarah, just so he'd know that she shared my attitude.

We passed through Customs without any hassle, stopped by what I would call a coffee shop except that no one there had clearly ever heard of coffee (or muffins, or biscuits), ate just enough to stop us from waking up hungry in the middle of the night, and then walked over to the desk of the small spaceport hotel.

The clerk was an eight-foot-tall Torqual. Like Novera, he had a nose on each side of his head, but much of the resemblance ended there—apparently not all Torquals were muscle-bound freaks.

"Good evening," he said in Cartheeli. "Welcome to Renceeti. I hope you will enjoy your stay here. It's a beautiful place."

"It looked lovely from above," said Keelarah.

"It is every bit as beautiful on the ground," he replied. Suddenly something beeped inside his left ear, and he closed his eyes for a moment, frowning in concentration. Finally he looked across at us. "I am told you have requested a somewhat irregular sleeping arrangement."

"One room, two beds," I said in Terran. "Nothing unusual about that."

It must have been the tone of my voice, because he nodded his head vigorously and said, also in Terran, "Yes, sir, absolutely nothing." He fiddled with his computer for a few seconds. "You are in Room 317, overlooking the small lake just behind the hotel."

"How do we reach it?" I asked.

He pointed at a well-lit rectangular shaft. "The airlift over there, sir."

"And how do we get into the room?" asked Keelarah.

"Customs has already given me your retina readings, which have been programmed into the door. Further, if you have not been drinking *xchhom*, you can merely exhale on the door and it will recognize the breaths unique to your bodies and open for you."

"And we lock it how?" I asked. He gave me a suspicious look. "Just in case we want to sleep late and not be disturbed by the maintenance robots."

"Not a problem, sir," he answered. "They are programmed never to enter an occupied room unless the occupant requests them."

"Fine," I said, as Keelarah left her thumbprint so they could transfer payment for the room from her account to theirs.

We walked over to the airlift, floated comfortably up to the third floor, and walked down the corridor to Room 317. I was going to let it read my retina, but Keelarah pushed me aside with a smile, then turned and blew at the door, which instantly opened.

"You look almost *too* amused," she said as I followed her into the room.

"There's an ancient nursery tale…" I began.

"Nursery tale?" she asked, frowning.

"Children's fable," I explained. "About three little pigs, and a wolf that blows their door down, or tries to, I can't remember which. And don't ask what a wolf or a pig is," I added with a smile. "They've been extinct for millennia."

She chuckled. "We have children's fables about talking animals too." She paused thoughtfully. "I suppose every race does."

We suddenly heard a heavy thudding above us.

"I guess they put all the thousand-pounders on the fourth floor," I said.

"It makes sense," she replied.

"You know something about the fourth floor that I don't?" I asked her.

She shook her head. "No," she said. "I meant that probably each floor was designed, constructed, and furnished to fit one particular type or size of being."

"I suppose so," I said, pointing at the beds. "Even the desk clerk couldn't fit in that, let alone the critter that was pounding the floor above us."

She sat down on a heavily-padded chair. "This is more comfortable than you might think."

I tried one that was facing her. "Not bad," I admitted.

She was silent for a moment, then frowned. "I'm still annoyed at that leering creature at the spaceport," she said. "And if his insinuations weren't bad enough, he was a *Cartheeli*."

"If he wasn't, he probably wouldn't have given a damn," I said.

"He's an idiot with a one-track mind!" she snapped.

"A lot of members of that gender, regardless of their race or species, tread on that same track," I said. "That's how we keep the universe populated."

"I know," she said distractedly. "But you're a human and I'm…"

"What you are is a kind, beautiful person," I said, "and that's not limited to race or gender."

"Thank you," she said. "Forgive me for forgetting even for a moment what a *dhomax* you are."

"A *dhomax*?" I repeated, frowning.

She smiled. "You would say a gentleman."

I returned her smile. "Not a lot of people have ever called me a gentleman," I said. "Especially not of your gender."

She got to her feet and walked the three steps to my chair. "But you are," she said. "You are the most thoughtful male I have ever encountered."

"Including pod-mates, or whatever you call them?"

"Including everyone," she said, bending over and running her extraordinarily soft, smooth tongue across my forehead.

I reached out, grabbed her arm, and gently pulled her down to where she was sitting crossways on my lap. She looked at me questioningly, but made no move to get away, and I kissed her full upon the lips.

"I have read about that in some of your literature while you were asleep on the ship," she said. "That is a kiss, is it not?"

"Yes," I said. "Pretty much what you did to me."

"We call that a *myirl*," she said. "Did you like it?"

"I liked the thought behind it," I said.

"But the *feel*?" she persisted.

I shrugged. "Pleasant. What about you? Did you like being kissed?"

"I liked the fact that you want to show affection to me."

"But that was it?"

She shrugged helplessly. "We are different races."

I nodded my head sadly. "I know, Greenie. And we just proved it again."

"I know that I love you," she said. "I love you with all my heart. But as a sardonic Fate would have it, I cannot love you with all my body."

"Ditto," I said.

"Ditto?" she repeated, frowning.

"It means: exactly the same," I replied.

"I wish it could be different," said Keelarah, and for a being that I had never seen cry before, a tear rolled down her cheek for the third time in just a couple of days.

"So do I," I said. "But I'll settle for being grateful for what I have."

She held my hand in hers, and we remained motionless for the next hour, each thinking our own thoughts, which probably weren't that unique anyway, until it was finally time to go to bed, separated by perhaps twenty feet and half a galaxy.

FOURTEEN

We were up at sunrise. Not that we slept all that well, each finally coming to grips with the reality of our situation, but whatever was in the room above us made more noise pounding across the floor than a parade of elephants.

I was curious to see if something that *sounded* so huge could actually fit in the airlift, but though I insisted we stand by the lift to get a look at him (or it, or whatever), he'd either gone downstairs already or was back in bed now that he'd kept half of the third floor awake.

We skipped breakfast—no great sacrifice, given the menu—and then arranged for a sightseeing tour of the nearby countryside. The vehicle had a robotic driver who was programmed to answer all our questions as well as point out everything we were seeing, and due to a last minute cancellation by a couple of Myrtors we didn't have to share it with anyone.

It was as pretty as it had looked from the air. Everything was in blossom, everything smelled fresh, the water was clear enough that we could see gold-hued alien fish swimming around, and now and then we'd see a small herd of local herbivores that looked a lot like six-legged goats grazing on the hillside.

"It's just lovely!" enthused Keelarah after perhaps an hour.

"Is any of this land for sale?" I asked. "I haven't seen anything resembling a house or a barn."

"No, no one may live beyond the limits of the various cities," answered the robot. "We take great pride in our wilderness and we intend to keep it pure and pristine."

I gave it a moment's thought, and then said: "That means you import all your food from other worlds."

"That is correct," said the robot.

"So a steak—we won't even argue what kind of animal it comes from—that costs me ten credits on a similar world one or two systems away might cost me seventy-five credits here?"

"Sixty-eight, I believe, sir," replied the robot.

"And the same with raw materials for houses?"

"We do not permit new houses, sir," said the robot. "You must buy an existing structure."

"And if it needs repair, I cannot use local woods or metals?" I persisted.

"That is correct, sir."

I turned to Keelarah. "Golden Dream, hell," I said with a grim smile. "This one is Platinum Dream."

"At the very least," she concurred. "Though in a way I admire the government's desire to keep it as pristine as possible."

"The government needs more money than you think to keep it this way."

"Oh?" she said. "You sound like you speak with authority, yet I know you haven't spoken to any member of the government or contacted them through your computer."

"I don't have to," I said.

"Please explain," said Keelarah.

"You paid for our room. If it was outrageously out of the ordinary, I'm sure your bank, whatever world it's on, would have informed you by now. I bought us dinner. Forget whether it was good or mediocre, what it was was reasonably priced."

"I don't follow you," she said, frowning.

"It's all a come-on, Keelarah," I said. "From what little we've learned about this place from the robot, that meal should have cost ten times as much. Same with the room. Even this sight-seeing excursion was what I would call reasonable. Yet we know that they have to import *everything*, from food to building materials to computers. It costs a fortune to run a planet that operates on this principle, and there's only one place to get the fortune: from the citizenry."

"Maybe they have some immense diamond mine or something similar," she said.

"The day word got out, do you think they'd still be a peaceful little world with no military and almost no immigrants?"

Keelarah shook her head. "No," she said. "No, I suppose not."

"Well, we can complete the tour," I said, "and vacation as long as you want, or we can go back to the hotel, check out, and have Jesse take us to the next world."

She sighed deeply. "We'll go back, of course."

"I'm as disappointed as you are," I said. "For the first few minutes we were driving, I was looking at each hill, each little lake and stream, and wondering: Is *that* where we should build our home?"

"I know," she said. "I was thinking the same thing."

"Well," I said, "what the hell. There's only twelve or fifteen billion more worlds."

"I hope we don't have to look at all of them," she said with a bitter smile.

"Oh, we'll find something, some place, pretty soon," I assured her.

But I was beginning to wonder.

FIFTEEN.

We hit nine worlds in the next fifteen days. A few had inhospitable climates, a couple had inadequate atmosphere for long-term living (by which I mean atmospheric contents, not social milieus), one had heavy enough gravity that we were exhausted just walking from the ship to the Customs building.

But what we noticed most often were the disapproving looks we received when it became clear that we were traveling together, rather than two strangers sharing the same transportation.

It was very strange. I certainly wouldn't mind if a Proxote traveled or lived with a Malachor, any more than I'd mind if a collie played with a cocker spaniel. After all, I'd never gone to war, no human had, with any of them in all our recorded history.

But we were getting those looks from everyone, the few humans and Cartheelis we met, plus damned near every other race. I could almost hear them thinking *"Perverts!"* as we'd walk past.

There were no out-and-out scenes. Restaurants all sat and served us—slowly. Hotels and boarding houses accommodated us—reluctantly. Drivers and tour guides showed off their worlds to us—unenthusiastically.

I was getting madder and madder. At one hotel I felt a heavy weight on my arm, and realized that it was Keelarah practically swinging on it. I questioned her about it after we reached our room and the door closed behind us.

"You were going to hit that Toboni," she said.

"The clerk?"

"Yes."

"I didn't like the way he was looking at us," I told her.

"He didn't say anything."

"He didn't have to."

"Please," she said. "Just getting through the day on some of these worlds is hard enough. Please don't hit or otherwise antagonize any of them. When you really think about it, they're nothing to us."

"Look," I said, "they can say anything they want to me. Whatever it is, I've heard worse, both in warfare and in basic training. But when they look at *you* with contempt, or say something I don't like to *us*..."

"That's when you must exercise self-control, Brown."

"Sonuvabitch was just asking for it," I growled.

"And if you'd hit him, what then?"

"I'd have felt a hell of a lot better, and he'd have learned a lesson in manners," I said.

She shook her head. "You would have been arrested and thrown in jail, and I'd have been alone on an alien world that clearly has no love for the Cartheeli."

I stared at her for a long minute. "I hadn't considered that," I admitted at last.

"Please *start* considering it."

"I will," I promised her.

She walked over and hugged me. "I know you will," she said.

"I'm sorry things aren't going more smoothly, Greenie."

"Is there no world that wants us?" she said plaintively. "No place where we can be happy?"

I looked down at her and kissed her cheek.

"There's always the next place," I said.

SIXTEEN.

We didn't have much luck at the next place, or the place after that.

"Jesse," I said when we'd returned to the ship after another unhappy incident—Bareimus III was a world that had just enough experience with humans not to want any to settle there, with or without an alien companion—"get us the hell out of this section."

"Where do you wish me to go?" it asked.

"I don't know," I muttered. "At least a couple of hundred light years away."

"In which direction?"

"North, south, I don't care," I said.

"North and south are not meaningful terms when traversing the void," Jesse lectured me.

"Okay," I said. "Find an area between two hundred and two hundred twenty-five light years from here with at least five habitable planets in a ten-light-year range."

"Checking my star maps. Checking my database. Done."

And with that, we changed directions slightly and began accelerating.

"I will enter the Durjeenih Wormhole in seventeen minutes," Jesse announced.

"Good," I said, "Warn us again a minute before you reach it."

"Yes, Chip."

I turned to Keelarah, who had been sitting there quietly. "He's becoming so damned human, I half expect him to say 'Aye aye, sir!' instead of 'Yes, Chip'."

"Do you think it will be any different where we're going?" she asked, ignoring my remark.

"Sooner or later it has to be," I said.

"I really thought we'd found a place," she said sadly.

I frowned. "Bareimus?"

She shook her head. "No, of course not. We never even got past Customs there. I mean Steipe IV."

"It was a pretty world," I said. "Good gravity, weather, oxygen, everything."

"Except their laws," she added.

I grimaced and nodded my agreement. They hadn't minded that two species had traveled there together, but were quick to point out that their law forbade different species from cohabiting together. I pointed out that we were not married, we were incapable of producing offspring (I left out the part about being incapable of having sex), and that we were just friends who had shared a ship and now planned to share a dwelling. It didn't do a bit of good, and when they rattled off the size of the fines and prison sentences for breaking that particular law we took our leave of them.

"I just don't understand it," I muttered. "How the hell hard can it be?"

"Harder than we thought," replied Keelarah. "Maybe a thousand years ago, when thousands of empty planets were first being colonized…"

"But it makes no sense!" I snapped. "These idiot laws and customs came about to prevent us from doing something we're physically incapable of doing in the first place!"

"Clearly others in our situation weren't incapable, and just as clearly the results, one way or another, were detrimental."

I sighed deeply. "I know, I know. And there's a million planets with the right conditions out there for the taking—but I'm not a housebuilder or a farmer or—"

"Calm yourself, Brown," said Keelarah. "We've only tried a mere handful of worlds. There are thousands, probably tens of thousands, of populated worlds. We just have to be patient."

I didn't reply, because I knew she was right. I pulled up the star charts and started considering which of the worlds in the area we were traveling to seemed the likeliest.

I couldn't have been more wrong about the first two.

And then we came to a little world with the thoroughly unmemorable name of Pano V.

SEVENTEEN

"I just can't face another world that won't have us, or where we won't fit," said Keelarah as we touched down. "Would you mind terribly if I stayed on the ship and let you check it out yourself?"

"No, of course not," I said. "I'll be back in an hour, maybe less if I see problems right away." I turned to the hatch. "Open it up, Jesse."

"Yes, Chip," said the ship. "You won't need any breathing equipment, and the gravity is only eight percent greater than Standard."

"Sounds good," I said. "Keep a watch for me and open the hatch again when you see me coming back."

"Yes, Chip."

Then I was outside, climbing down the six stairs to the ground, and walking to Customs. They cleared me instantly, and fortunately the spaceport was a part of the town, so I didn't have to hunt for public transportation.

The place seemed pleasant enough. I didn't see any humans or Cartheelis, but there were fifteen or twenty various races, most pretty much humanoid in appearance. I walked around for about half an hour, and after I turned back, headed to Customs and then to the ship to tell Keelarah that Pano V had possibilities, I came to a tavern.

I was studying the bottles on display in the window, wondering if any of them would be acceptable to my system, when

I heard a scream and a crash from inside. A second later a smallish humanoid figure, about five feet tall, with huge orange eyes and an elongated foreface, rushed out the door, damned near bumped into me, then turned to his left and raced away between buildings.

The bartender was next out the door, yelling the equivalent of "Stop, thief!" and then running back inside, probably to summon the police.

I decided that doing a good deed might be just the thing to put me—and my Greenie, of course—in good standing with the community in case we decided to settle here, so I stealthily began following the thief between the buildings. The open area led through to the next street, and when I got there I saw him entering a dilapidated building a block away.

I saw no need to lurk in the shadows and proceed as cautiously as he did, so I just walked down the metallic ramp that passed for a sidewalk, totally out in the open, until I came to the building. I checked to make sure he didn't have any confederates waiting in the shadows behind the door, ready to shoot or pounce on me, and then I entered.

"Hold it right there," said a voice in accented Terran.

I turned to my left and found myself facing the small humanoid, who was pointing a burner at me.

"That's far enough," he said. "You police or syndicate?"

I frowned. "Syndicate?"

"The critters that run half the joints in town."

"Critters?" I repeated. "I like your choice of language."

"So you're police."

I shook my head, then realized that he might not know what that meant. "No, I don't work for anyone."

"Then why did you follow me?" he said. "I saw you when I ran out of the tavern."

"You want the truth?" I said.

"Can't be any harder to believe than most of the lies I've heard."

For a being that wasn't born to use Terran, I liked the way he handled it. It sounds strange to relate, since he was holding a gun on me, but I found myself almost liking him.

"My friend and I are—"

"Where is he?" he interrupted, turning his burner on the doorway for a moment.

"On my ship, and it's a *she*," I said. "We've been looking for a world to live on. Tried maybe a dozen, maybe a few more than that, and couldn't stay on any of them."

"You're very picky," he said with what I took to be a smile.

"Not as picky as most of the worlds were," I answered.

"Oh? Tell me about it."

"Nothing much to tell. We'd find a world with conditions we could both take, and there was always some reason not to stay."

"Let me guess," he said. "She's not a human."

"She's a Cartheeli."

"Whatever the hell *they* are."

"So I thought if I apprehended you, did a good deed for the local society, they might prove to be a little friendlier or more lenient than the last few worlds."

"And do you still plan to apprehend me?" he asked in what I assume were amused tones.

I shook my head. "No," I said.

"Might I ask why not?"

"This is going to sound strange since we've only know each other for about two minutes," I replied, "but I already like the way you talk and think."

He smiled again, and this time I *knew* it was a smile. "I'm kind of fond of you myself," he said. "My name's Rozotet. What's yours?"

"Forrest."

"Pleased to meet you, Forrest," he said. "I'd stay and visit, but..."

"Yeah, I understand," I said. "The gendarmes are coming."

He shook his head. "Not a chance," he replied with certainty. "No one saw where I went except you."

"Then what's your hurry?" I asked, because in truth I was enjoying the conversation, strange as that may seem.

"The female I live with is very ill," said Rozotet. "Without her medications there's a chance she could die—and this is the closest world to where we live that has the required medication. It is both rare and expensive, and I didn't have the money to pay for it." Suddenly he flashed me another smile. "And I'd rather rob a tavern that could care less about me than a pharmacy that can save her life."

"Makes sense to me," I agreed. "Just out of curiosity, what kind of illness does your race tend to come down with?"

He shrugged. "Nothing, really."

"But—" I began.

"She is not my race."

"I take it you live on *your* planet, since her medication is so scarce."

"No," he said. "We don't live on either of our home planets, probably for the same reasons you and your lady don't. We live on Xylor."

"Never heard of it."

"That's the name of the first settler, the first guy to even attempt to map it," he explained. "It's on your star maps as Trentichi III."

"And you have no…ah…*social* difficulties living there?"

"None." Suddenly he smiled. "Our entire planetary population is just over three thousand—and this includes members of more than six hundred races. Hell, we've even got a human or two living there."

"Really?"

"The atmosphere and gravity doesn't bother them, and they certainly have no trouble eating what they grow. They haven't broken any laws." Suddenly he smiled again. "Not that we've got any to break."

"Must keep your police force busy," I opined.

"Haven't got one," replied Rozotet. "On Xylor you protect what's yours—and most of the residents are more than capable of doing just that."

"How far away is this Xylor?" I asked.

He frowned and thought for a moment. "Maybe seven light years," he answered at last. "But get out beyond our moons and the Gruvonni Wormhole can get you there in about two hours."

"You make it sound…*interesting*," I said, trying not to sound too enthused or excited.

He shrugged. "It's really very boring," he said. "No mountains, no rolling plains, straight unimaginative rivers, same climate year around."

"But you choose to live there," I noted.

"Sure," he said. "For the same reason every other resident does."

"And that reason is…?"

"It abounds in one quality that you won't find on your star maps," said Rozotet.

"Oh?" I said.

He nodded. "Tolerance." He walked to the door. "And now I must go."

"Perhaps I'll see you again," I said.

"I hope so," he replied.

"I hope so too," I said.

And then he was gone.

EIGHTEEN

The ship touched down on Xylor.

"All right," said Keelarah, looking out the porthole at the dull, brown landscape. "Why here?"

"Just a hunch," I said.

"Where's the Customs building?" she asked, then began looking around. "In fact, where's the spaceport?"

"There isn't any," I said.

"On the whole planet?"

"That's my understanding," I replied.

"What's the resident race?" she asked.

"Beats the hell out of me," I said. "Why not ask Jesse?"

"All right," she said. "Jesse, you heard my question."

"There is no resident race," answered the ship. "This was a totally unpopulated planet ninety-three Standard years ago."

"Okay," she said. "What's the dominant race?"

"There is none," said the ship.

"You're driving me crazy," she muttered. "What is the most numerous race?"

"For the moment, Torquals."

"What do you mean: for the moment?" demanded Keelarah.

"There are nineteen Torquals," responded Jesse. "But there are seventeen Prouvettes, and one of them is due to hatch a litter of four sometime next week."

She frowned. "Nineteen, seventeen? Just how the hell many races are there on this world?"

"Six hundred and forty-seven at the moment," said the ship.

She turned to me. "You knew this?"

I nodded.

"You've met one of them," she said with certainty.

"Rozotet," I answered. "Seemed like a pleasant enough guy." I did not add, "For a thief."

"Is he the one who's waiting for a hatching?"

I shook my head. "He and his partner are in the same situation we're in. In fact, I want to look in on him in a day or two. She's quite ill. I met him while he was...procuring medications for her."

"And they've had no problems?"

"None."

"And no one else has either?"

"Evidently not," I answered.

"Jesse, open the hatch," said Keelarah.

It opened, and she climbed down to the ground, where I joined her a moment later.

"Isn't that odd?" she said at last.

"Isn't *what* odd?" I asked.

"The ground is brown, the sky is blue, the lake over there is gray, that small ridge is covered with something kind of reddish." She looked up at a pair of avians flying overhead. "They're pink and tan."

"So?"

She smiled up at me. "Whoever thought that Golden Dream would come in every color except gold?"

WHAT CAME BEFORE

WHEN PARALLEL LINES MEET

PREQUEL

FAMILY DREAMS

LARRY HODGES

ONE

Forrest Brown was eight when his parents launched him into space, alone in a tiny escape pod, with little hope for survival. Roving insectoid aliens known as the Witheroo had attacked his parents' mining station. Forrest's last memory of the station was of collapsing walls and roofs, with fire and smoke everywhere as his dad practically threw him into the pod while his mom tossed in food and bottled water. Then they closed the lid, and within seconds he was soaring through the smoke into space. He stared out the viewscreen at the station, the only home he'd ever known.

Then it exploded.

Forrest was alone, in the asteroid belt of the Vandolian system, one hundred million miles from the planet Vandolia, a human military base. Alone, drifting through space, with no chance of rescue or survival once basis supplies ran out. Alone to die.

Except he wasn't alone. Minutes after the explosion a monstrous face appeared outside the viewscreen. It was brown and diamond shaped, covered by a transparent spherical space helmet. A pair of huge, multifaceted eyes stared in at him. They moved independently of each other as they looked about his capsule, with one of them occasionally glancing back at where the station had once been. Trailing out behind the helmet was a long, stick-like body, exposed to space, with eight trailing legs. Tied to its back was a cylinder that occasionally shot out mist as the Witheroo maneuvered about the pod.

A survivor. The thought appeared in Forrest's head. *A little human. I'd like to question you before you die.*

Why? Forrest thought back.

Knowledge must be gathered before it is lost. Your people stole rock from a sacred place, and so we killed them, but knowledge is neither good nor evil, merely something to collect.

What do you want to know?

I must learn all that you know. The alien stared into Forrest's eyes as he stared back, transfixed, unable to look away. Then Forrest grimaced, and pulled his eyes back, breaking the trance.

"Get the hell off my spaceship!" he cried. He punched the viewscreen where the alien appeared, but only injured his fist.

The alien projected a mental smile. Then a light shot from its head to Forrest's, invisible to the boy's eyes but somehow visible in his mind. Forrest cried out as it seared painfully into his brain, which felt like it was turning inside out as memories, even long forgotten ones, were squeezed out, like a hundred thousand movies played simultaneously at ten times normal speed, then a hundred, and then just a whir.

When it ended, Forrest stared back at the Witheroo, his memories gone. His memory began only minutes before, with his parents putting him into the escape pod. Everything before that was a blank. Then the Witheroo began to suck that last memory out. Forrest felt it leaving through the light beam. He fought it, willing the memories to stay, but they pulled away, becoming less a memory and more a dream.

A boring life, thought the alien. *But the knowledge will live forever, and in a way, so shall you, even after I destroy your escape pod.*

There was another explosion from where the space station had once been, perhaps some leftover part that had survived the previous explosion. One of the alien's eyes glanced back at the explosion even as the other continued to stare at Forrest as his last memories were pulled from him. Forrest stared back.

As Forrest stared into the unblinking eye of the alien, something large from the explosion smashed into it like a bus at a thousand miles per hour. One instant the alien was staring at him, the next it was gone.

Once again Forrest was alone. Except once again he wasn't quite alone. Something from the alien had stayed inside his head, along with the dreamlike memory of his last minutes on the space station and his time with the Witheroo. At first it was like a painful thorn in the side of his brain. Then it sank into it and became a part of it.

How long Forrest floated in space he'd never know. The escape pod was truly small, built for a child even smaller than Forrest. He began to panic, and pounded his fists on the viewscreen. He needed to get out of this tiny prison! Over and over he punched and kicked out, but the cocoon-like escape pod was built to withstand a pounding far greater than anything a child could inflict.

Then he screamed with his mind, and beams of light shot out in all directions. Like the alien's beam of light, they were invisible to the eye—and by this time Forrest's eyes were tightly closed in fear—but he could see them in his mind as they shot out at light speed, cries of terror and distress.

One of them reached the Vandolian world. By then it was stretched out into a wider beam thousands of feet across, but when it hit a city, hundreds of Vandolians shared his terror and distress. Soon a Vandolian rescue ship was on its way.

He had no memories from before his parents put him on the escape pod, which a Vandolian psychiatrist attributed to shock, and incorrectly predicted would return. Sadly, he also had little memory of what his mom or dad looked like; they had spent their lives in the back worlds and mining stations, and when their mining station blew up, so did all known pictures of them. All he remembered of them were dreamlike images as they packed him into the escape pod. However, he would never forget the alien, especially those last few seconds as he stared into its eye, and that instant when it was smashed aside.

But mostly he remembered floating in space, seemingly forever, in that tiny prison of an escape pod.

TWO

Nothing sucks more than growing up in an orphanage. Nothing prepares you for life more. That's what Forrest told himself during those boring years growing up on Vandolia, third planet from the sun and about as earthlike a planet as was possible. The only things that made it bearable were the Museum of Man, and Mop the bronto.

Wherever Man goes, he brings his culture, and Vandolia, with its growing population, was no exception. The Museum of Man was a five-minute walk from the orphanage. The first time Forrest went in was out of curiosity. What could possibly be of interest in a dusty old museum to a nine year old? Even the search computer was worn out from years of use, mostly by older patrons. Just for laughs, Forrest put in his name. His eyebrows shot up with surprise and interest when he saw all the results. He'd never known another Forrest before; now he saw there were many others, plus places and even books with the name. Before he left he downloaded a copy of an old book called *Forrest Gump*. A week later he was back, reading all he could of that time period. Soon he was the planet's top authority on the culture of twentieth century Earth after reading *The Maltese Falcon* and other books from the time, about the Roswell aliens—first contact, though few knew about it at the time—and about sports stars of the time, such as Babe Ruth, Wilt Chamberlain, and Jesse Owens. There was little literature for many years after that time period due to the nuclear wars of the following century that led to centuries of darkness.

Mop the bronto, in a bright red sweater, had zero knowledge of ancient Man. But she enjoyed a good game of Mips and Kips, which in Terran translates to Boulders and Pebbles, which was basically hide and seek, with the giant bronto children trying to find the hiding human children. One of the hiding human children was Forrest, desperately trying to hide under a fallen log. The other children had disappeared into tunnels and crevices under real boulders.

Loud footsteps approached, with the ground shaking with each footfall. Forrest curled into a ball, trying to make himself as small as possible. Then the log came crashing down about him as it broke into pieces under the mass of the giant leg and many tons of mass. In a panic, he sent out a mental signal, *Don't see me!* The psych powers he'd gotten from the Witheroo only worked under stress, and didn't work well on the brontos.

"I see you!" said the deep, slow voice of Mop in Terran. "You are like a little chip of wood!"

"Get your smelly feet away from me!" Forrest cried.

"Okay, little chip!" said Mop. There was twittering laughter from the nearby tunnels and crevices. Mop went still, listening, and then lowered her long neck to the nearest tunnel. She went in like a giant snake, and a moment later came out, a small, wriggling boy in her jaws. She placed him on the ground, and said, "Got you!"

The boy jumped to his feet, pointed at Forrest, and said, "Hi, Chip!" and then ran off. And from there on, Forrest was Chip to his friends and tormentors.

"Why didn't you hide in one of the tunnels?" asked Mop. "The log didn't hide you very well. Plus, I almost stepped on you."

"I don't like small places," Chip said.

"Why not?"

"It's a long story."

"I have a long time. I'm tired of this game."

"Would you like to see the Museum of Man?" he asked, to change the subject. She nodded, and they walked over. It wasn't built for brontos, but she squeezed her way in. Soon Forrest was reading her the adventures of Forrest Gump and his girlfriend, Jenny. "I think I will call you Jenny," he said.

"That sounds nice," said Mop, now Jenny. "I wasn't happy to discover my name in Terran was a cleaning device."

Mop was also nine, and soon they became companions as they grew into adulthood. Brontos were the dominant life-form on Vandolia, at least until Man arrived. They were dinosaurian creatures of the saurian kind, stuck for apparently thousands of years in an intellectually enlightened but pre-industrial civilization—lots of great music and literature, but no machines or advanced weaponry. They dominated the warmer areas of the planet, but avoided the colder regions in the north and south. They had long ago hunted down the meat-eating species, which now only existed in zoos. The brontos and their kin were a classic case of parallel evolution, only on this world, instead of a battle of tooth and claw, it had been thousands of years of peace and harmony.

And then Man, in his eternal quest for dominance, established a base in the north. It had started out as a small human military outpost for the Terran Confederation, but after the discovery of mineral deposits in the system's asteroid belt, there had been a mineral rush, and soon it had grown into a prosperous city of over a hundred thousand, which they called, quite simply, The City of Man. Mining was a dangerous profession, forcing the creation of the orphanage. The sociable brontos, wearing huge knit sweaters made by humans, often visited the region, with some of them staying, and so Forrest got to know them and their Vandolian language.

THREE

"What do you want to do when you grow up?" Jenny asked, jumping interchangeably from Terran to Vandolian and back. She and Chip were now fourteen.

"I don't know," Chip admitted. "Maybe get a wife, have a couple of kids, get a job, and live to a ripe old age." He sat on her back as she walked back from their visit to the newly created Museum of Brontos. He wondered if it was an omen that they were already turning the dominant lifeform into a museum piece.

"But what do *you* want to do?" she asked. "Are you going to spend the rest of your life on Vandolia, getting old as you and your kind take over the planet?"

Chip grimaced to himself. Over the past five years humans had discovered mineral deposits throughout much of the warmer regions. The brontos lived mostly on the coasts, by the major waterways, which were needed for local transportation of these minerals, and slowly the brontos had been pushed out of the coastal regions as Man created settlements all over the world.

"I definitely want to get off this rock," Chip said. "Maybe I could be an explorer and find a new world for the brontos."

"You want to find a home for us instead of our home here, on Vandolia?" Jenny asked, smiling as only a bronto could, with lips thicker than a human thigh. "Why not find a home for humans instead?"

But there seemed only one way off of Vandolia, and that was the military. Chip took the usual required military training courses in school, but gave little thought to an actual military career.

And then, on the day he turned eighteen, he was drafted.

FOUR

B oot camp is the same everywhere and everywhen, and it was the same for Chip. Shaved heads, check. Sadistic sergeant; check. Early morning and late night runs with full backpack, check. Hours and hours of push-ups, sit-ups, rope-climbing, obstacle-course running, and other silly exercises that had little to do with modern high-tech warfare, check. Hand-to-hand combat training just in case the enemy showed up without burners, check. Taking apart and putting back together your burner blindfolded while the sadistic sergeant slapped you silly while calling your mother names, in the off chance you lose your burner in battle and find a disassembled one lying on the ground and have to put it together while an enemy soldier slaps you silly and calls your mother names, check.

Eventually they did get to actually use the burner, and Chip found he was a pretty good shot. He progressed from hand to rifle to bazooka burners. He also learned all about tactical warfare, especially in regard to humanity's newest mortal enemy, the telepathic Witheroo. But with protective helmets, their mental powers were nullified. Chip kept his own minor telepathic powers to himself. He had little control over them anyway, and if those in charge knew his secret, he'd spend the rest of his life in some institution with scientists looking for an excuse to dissect his brain.

After boot camp, Chip and his unit were assigned to the front lines in battle after battle as they took over the Witheroo empire, one system at a time. He'd already lost two families, and had no interest in gaining and losing a third, so he mostly kept to himself—and when his fellow soldiers died, one by one, he only drew more into himself. He saw more death than he'd ever want to think about, often in times of high stress, where he'd feel the fear and agony as the Witheroo and fellow humans died.

Three times he was almost killed, and all three times his psych powers, only present under such high stress, saved him. The Witheroo were totally unprepared for a human with such powers. Whenever a Witheroo was about to kill him, Chip would mentally lash out, they'd freeze up, and it would be the last thing they would do as Chip or one of his fellow soldiers killed the alien with their burners.

After ten short years the only Witheroo left alive were herded onto reservations on their own planet, now ruled by humans, who began the systematic removal of mineral and other forms of wealth. The glorious war had been won; long live the human race! Chip had served two glorious five-year terms for the Terran Confederation. With no more war, it was time to go home.

Vandolia was no longer the world he remembered. Once the mineral wealth of Vandolia was realized, Man had taken over the planet with amazing speed. The coastal regions had become giant cities that stretched for hundreds of miles along the oceans and seas. About half the brontos had survived the Wars of Destiny. They had been herded into reservations in less desirable lands, just like the Witheroo.

Chip found Jenny on one such reservation...or at least what was left of her. Her tail and one eye were missing. Her front right leg had been shot off, and had been replaced with a poorly-fitted manmade prosthetic. When Chip found her, the two at first just stared at each other. Then Jenny lowered her head, and Chip hugged her. She nudged him in the side, then rose back to her full height.

"You should leave," she said. "This is no longer our world, neither is it yours."

Chip had already read about the wars, and had little to say.

"Go," she said. "You are my friend, but you are also my enemy."

He left, returning to the spaceport, and would never see her again.

But where was he to go? He had enough credits saved from his military years that he was in no rush. But he had no home, no family, not even a homeworld. All he knew was the Vandolia of the past, and a military life he now rejected.

No family, he thought to himself. He looked about the busy spaceport and wondered how many others were like him, without so much as a vestige of a family. He saw what appeared to be a mother scolding two children as a grim-faced father stood over them, no doubt wondering whether to take off his belt and use it. They had no idea how good they had it. He felt that there was nothing left for him but to go back to the military. Another five-year tour? He shuddered. But it would be so easy—Vandolia was still, at least in theory, primarily a military base, and there was a military office right here at the spaceport. He began walking toward it. Better to let them take care of his future than him worry about it.

At the entrance, he hesitated. Did he really want to do this? Again? But what other options did he have? Sighing, he entered.

"I'd like to re-enlist," he said to the sergeant at the desk, who looked him over with a military-issued painted-on smile.

"This'll just take a minute," the sergeant said. He handed Chip a palm computer. A minute later Chip's info was on the screen, he'd checked off *re-enlist*, and only had to sign it with the attached digital pen. As usual in times of high stress, his psych powers swung into action, and he could almost hear the sergeant saying in his mind, *Sign it! Sign it!*

"I don't know," Chip said, pondering. And then he felt something else, a panic that didn't come from the man at the desk. Confused, he looked about.

Then came the screeching that changed his life.

"*Stop that monkey!*" someone yelled. Something small, brown, and very loud shot in through the door, a blur of chittering motion as it jumped off the floor, shot into the air, and grabbed a lighting fixture in the ceiling. For a split second Chip saw the monkey's wide green eyes staring at him. It was two feet tall with a little red cap held on its head by a string around its chin. Then it spun about, turning its back on him—and once again Chip was face to face with the monkey, which didn't make sense. Then it dropped to the floor, and looked about for a second. Chip could feel its terror, but was bewildered as the creature faced one way and then the other, and that's when Chip realized it had a face on each side of its overly large head.

Then it leaped onto the desk as the sergeant threw up his hands to protect his face. The monkey screamed, staring at the door with one of its faces.

"Don't let it get away!" cried a very large man at the entrance. He slammed the door closed, thereby trapping the monkey. He pointed a rod at the monkey, and a thin thread shot out even as the monkey tried to dive off the desk. The thread hit it in mid-jump, and the tased monkey screamed even louder, and then went still as it fell behind the desk onto the floor.

"You lose something?" the sergeant asked as he picked up the limp body and put it back on the desk.

"That's my Carmalite two-faced monkey," the very large man said. He produced a short leash attached to a collar, and put it around the monkey's neck. "Purebred. It's worth a lot."

"What the hell is wrong with you?" Chip yelled at the man. "Do you always taser your pets?"

"Only when they misbehave and try to escape," said the very large man, glancing down at Chip with a pair of piercing blue eyes below curly orange hair and a matching orange mustache.

"Escape this," Chip said as he punched the man in the face. The man cried out, and tried to punch back, but Chip had already grabbed his taser and tased the man. He screamed as he went down.

"Do you always taser innocent people?" asked the sergeant. He'd come from around his desk and was examining the fallen man, who groaned as he lay on the floor.

"Only when they misbehave," said Chip. He gently picked up the monkey, which was beginning to stir. Sure enough, it had a face on the back of its head, identical to the one in front.

"Let's see," the sergeant said, "we've got you for assault, theft of property—his taser—and aiding and abetting the escape of an exotic, expensive animal—that's about twenty years in the pen. The only question is if you signed the screen to re-enlist, and get tried in military court, or didn't sign, and get tried in civilian court."

"I didn't sign."

The sergeant punched a button on his desk, and there was a click from the door. "The door's locked, so you aren't going anywhere. So…you got a choice. You can wait here while I call in the civilian authorities. Or you can re-enlist, which gets me a commission, and we can quietly forget all this happened."

"So all you want is your commission?"

"Lots of soldiers finished their tours, and with the Witheroo war over, didn't re-enlist," the sergeant said. "We still need soldiers to police the captured areas, hunt down any left-over bands of Witheroo, and prepare for the next war. Oh, and they've doubled the commission, so I really need you to sign that thing."

Chip stared down at the monkey, which was now awake and staring up at him with one of its faces. "What is this thing?"

"As the man said, that's a genuine genetically created two-faced Carmalite monkey," said the sergeant. "Made from Rhesus macaques, the smartest monkey, with the second face added as a novelty for exotic pet owner wannabes. Super smart, even has its own language. Causing a lot of problems back on Earth because they're too smart, and some of them want their own world."

"How do you know so much about them?"

The sergeant clicked his heels and saluted. "Sergeant Juskers, formerly of the Galactic Surveying Division, at your service. They survey new worlds for possible terraforming, colonization, mining, and other uses. I was part of the new Resettlement Squad, for emerging intelligences like the Carmalite, when this happened." He pulled up his right pants leg, and revealed an artificial leg.

"So you're blackmailing me into re-enlisting, just for your commission?"

Sergeant Juskers clicked his heels and saluted again, smiling. "At *my* service, sir!"

Chip wanted to spit at the man, or worse. Before he could decide what to do, the monkey had leaped from the desk onto his shoulder…and began licking his face.

"Stop that!" he cried, giggling, but the monkey was relentless, licking him in the cheeks, eyes, nose, and mouth. It kept rotating its head so it could alternately lick him with the tongue from one of its mouths and then the other. Chip gave in to the assault.

"I think you've made a friend," the sergeant said.

"I think you're right," Chip said. Now the monkey, which weighed about twenty pounds, was hugging him around the neck while gently poking at his face with its long, prehensile tail. "Okay, I'll sign—but three conditions."

"Anything reasonable is fine, as long as I get my commission."

"One, I keep the monkey."

"What monkey? I don't see no monkey," said the grinning sergeant.

"Two, you put me in the Galactic Surveying Division, Resettlement Squad."

"Not a problem, I can put you in directly."

"And three, a complete and absolute pardon for this."

"For what?" the sergeant asked, looking confused.

Chip punched him in the face, and the sergeant joined the very large man on the floor.

FIVE

Once again Chip's knowledge of ancient literature from the Museum of Man came to the rescue. Over the years he'd read the entire Batman comic series, and remembered Harvey "Two-Face" Dent. And so he named the monkey Harvey.

Chip and Harvey were soon on a ship to Earth, the birthplace of mankind. He'd never been there and knew far more about ancient Earth than the present one. Their stomachs did flip-flops as they went through the wormhole to Sol, which Chip dreaded but expected, while Harvey could only chitter away at full speed, fighting the temporary restraints that kept him from bouncing about the compartment in terror. The face on the back of Harvey's head was his "sad" face, and during their wormhole travels he'd turn that one to Chip with a look of *Why are you doing this to me?* When they were back to normal space, he'd race about the bridge, grinning at Harvey mostly with his "happy" front face. When the monkey was overly happy or sad, both faces would reflect that.

And then they were there—circling Earth, awaiting a shuttle for the trip down. Chip drank black coffee and snacked on muffins as he watched Earth through the viewscreen. Somehow the view just didn't do justice to the majestic ones he'd seen on large-screen computer screens. Earth had had its day, but after a couple thousand years exploring the space, even an ancestral home becomes a bit tiresome and boring. On the shuttle trip down he grew bored watching, and spent the time reading and snuggling with Harvey.

Sergeant Juskers was true to his word in assigning Chip to the Resettlement Squad. But Juskers got his revenge, as Chip soon found out. He was assigned to report to Colonel Muhammad, Director of the Resettlement Squad.

"Captain Brown reporting for duty!" he called out as he stood in front of her desk, with Harvey in his arms simultaneously staring at both of them. Colonel Muhammad wore a black veil over her face and hair, so all that showed were two very dark eyes. Her hands were gloved with a scale-like pattern.

Apparently she didn't speak Terran. *"What are we doing here?"* asked the voice from a translator device on her desk. Chip had to shush Harvey, who was chittering away.

"I said I'm reporting for duty, sir," Chip said.

Again Harvey began chittering as Colonel Muhammad spoke through the translating device. *"You shouldn't be here. You leave. Monkey leave. Both leave."*

Chip wasn't sure whether that was the way the Colonel really spoke, or if it was a problem with the translating device. He'd just arrived, and she wanted him to leave already?

"Sir, I think there's some mistake," Chip said. "I just arrived—"

"Leave now!" the translator device practically screamed, even as Harvey chittered equally loud.

"Sir—"

"Silence!" said a completely different voice, this time clearly coming from the veiled woman. "Are you through talking with your monkey?"

"Wait—you mean—"

"Yes, that was your monkey talking through my translator," said Colonel Muhammad. "You mean you didn't know they have their own language? And yet you think you'd qualify for the Resettlement Squad, whose job it is to find homes in the galaxy for these poor creatures?"

"I'm sorry, I didn't know—"

"That's 'I didn't know, *SIR!*'" Colonel Muhammad roared through her veil. "And there's a lot you don't know. I've heard all about you from Sergeant Juskers, about how you stole property from innocent civilians, tased this poor animal, and how he had to personally knock you out cold to get you to stop. I know the last place in the universe you want to be is here, in the Resettlement Squad, helping out these emerging intelligences, but guess what? I believe he was right in punishing you by assigning you here. Just remember this—I will have my eye on you. And I have my own taser." She pulled it from her belt for him to see. "I believe in an eye for an eye, and a taser for a taser. Don't make me use this. Now get out of my office and report back at 0800 tomorrow morning for acclimation."

So began Chip's career in the Galactic Surveying Division, Resettlement Squad.

SIX

"I talk to you all the time, you never answer," said Harvey in a high-pitched voice through Chip's tiny new translator, which Harvey wore on the string around his chin that held his red cap in place. He'd picked it up at the military supply hut after the episode in Colonel Muhammad's office.

"I didn't know you could speak. I don't speak Carmalite, it sounded like chittering, whistles, and grunts to me." Carmalite, it turned out, was an invented language for creatures without vocal cords, and was exactly what it sounded like—chittering, whistles, and grunts. Harvey could chitter from both faces, often at the same time when excited, but could only speak with the front face—apparently the back face wasn't connected to his brain's language processing center.

"Terran sound to me like gorilla whimpering. But still recognize it as language. Humans not smart. But still love you." He jumped up to grab Chip around the neck and planted a kiss on his cheek, and then hugged him. That night they pigged out on dinner, he on shrimp and lobster a la Newberg, an Earth delicacy, and Harvey on seven different types of fruit, including his favorite, banana watermelon.

The following morning they were back at Colonel Muhammad's office. She still wore her veil. "Pet breeders," she began without preamble, "in their infinite wisdom and stupidity, have bred intelligence into previously non-sentient beings. Three of them are now at near-human intelligence—"

"Above human!" corrected Harvey.

"—leading to major conflict. They have established their own colonies on Earth, but they just don't fit into the order of things—"

"Order of human things!" corrected Harvey.

"—and so some of them have armed themselves, leading to an escalating situation. The only answer, it seems, is to find them their own worlds. That is the purpose of the Resettlement Squad—to locate such worlds, and then resettle these emerging intelligences, thereby averting civil war—"

"Averting losing a war to a bunch of pets!" corrected Harvey.

"—and leading to peace and prosperity for all. Now, please stifle your monkey and follow me." She led them through a door in the back of her office, down a passageway, through another door and another passageway, and finally into a door marked *Office of the Ambassadors, Emerging Intelligences*. Inside was an empty office, with three doors in the back. She led them through the door on the left. Inside was a huge aquarium, with a giant blue fish floating at the top.

"This is the new embassy room of the dwarf *Balaenoptera musculus*," she said. "We haven't even put signs on their doors or the others."

"Where's the staff?" Chip asked, looking about the empty office as he breathed in the salty air, something he'd never experienced.

"I'm right here," said a deep, melodious voice in Terran. "The big blue fish." The fish was staring at them out of a tiny eye on the side of its head. The voice was coming from a hole in the top of its head, which was just out of the water.

"She's not really a fish," said Colonel Muhammad. "This is Ambassador Doby, the dwarf blue whale ambassador." The fish—Chip had a hard time thinking of it otherwise—was about eight feet long, bright blue, with a huge mouth that seemed in a perpetual smile, and a large flipper on each side of its body. It had a small dorsal fin, and large tail flukes which were sideways instead of the usual up and down of a normal fish.

"My ancestors were one hundred feet long and weighed 200 tons," Doby said. "But that's not convenient as a pet, so you magnificent humans genetically made us this tiny size, had our blueness and the silly smile on our face enhanced, and for hundreds of years our little selves made great pets for your wonderful boys and girls everywhere, who loved to poke us and stick their fat fingers in our blowholes. We live to serve! But then you decided to increase our intelligence, put vocal cords in our blowholes, and, well, here I am!" The eye looked side to side at each of them as they watched in stunned silence, then drooped downward. "Sorry."

"Is she for real, or is she being sarcastic?" asked Chip.

"I don't think Doby understands sarcasm," said Colonel Muhammad. "What you hear is what you get."

"We hate to go to war with you humans," said Ambassador Doby, "but, well, you are polluting the oceans a bit, so we don't really want to go back there, and you do keep us in these itty bitty aquariums. It'd be nice to find our own planet before we have to kill you all. Sorry. I promise I will try to represent my fellow dwarf blue whales on your journey to find our home-world. I hope I won't inconvenience you too much."

Next on the tour was the middle door. "This is the embassy of the Cottlesnakes," said Colonel Muhammad.

"I don't want to go there!" cried Harvey, staring at Chip with his sad face.

"Not sure if I want to either," said Chip.

"Actually, neither do I," said Colonel Muhammad. "But we're soldiers—"

"Speak for yourself!" cried Harvey.

"—and so danger does not deter us."

She opened the door, and they followed her in. Chip half expected an enormous snake mouth to reach down and swallow her whole as she struggled in its grasp—and wasn't let down much when a pair of jaws shot out of the shadows and swallowed her arm. The jaws were large enough to swallow a human if they stretched a bit, and behind the jaws was an overly large head with a pair of unblinking black eyes. The snake body behind that was perhaps fifteen feet long, a foot wide at its thickest. Colonel Muhammad held out a taser in her other arm and shocked the creature, which quickly spit out her arm. Blood trickled from two puncture wounds.

"You will die a poithoneth death," said the snake in Terran. Its neck had fanned out, showing the rough image of a human face. A rattling sound came from the large rattle on the end of its tail. Below the fanned-out neck the body was covered in thick green fur. Chip could dimly see a collage on the far wall of giant snakes swallowing people. The cool air smelled of spoiled meat.

"I had my anti-venom shots already," Colonel Muhammad said. She turned to Chip. "Cottlesnakes are warm-blooded, half cobra, half rattlesnake. Bred as an exotic pet, someone had the cute idea of giving them intelligence and vocal cords, but an inability to make the 's' sound. This is Ambassador Terror."

"I will eat you," said the snake. It swayed back and forth, looking for an opening with its huge, bulging eyes, but Colonel Muhammad kept the taser between them.

"This is their ambassador?" Chip asked.

"The others aren't as sociable," Colonel Muhammad explained. She pulled off one of her scale-covered gloves. One of her fingers was artificial. "I tried petting one of her children, and it bit me." She held up the glove. "I made this from its skin."

"My child, Anarchy, will embrathe you in her jawth in the afterlife," said Ambassador Terror.

"Can we leave now?" asked Harvey, shivering in Chip's arms.

"I think you can see why we'd like to find them their own homeworld," said Colonel Muhammad.

"Perhaps in Andromeda?" said Chip.

"Get uth off thith human infethted planet," said Ambassador Terror, "or remember thith: my anthethorth ate your anthethorth…and we are very hungry."

Harvey was already out the door, and the others quickly followed.

Colonel Muhammad pointed at the door on the far right. "This is the Carmalite Embassy."

"Finally!" Harvey exclaimed. He gave Chip a big kiss on the cheek. "I'm home!"

"Don't get too excited," said Colonel Muhammad. She opened the door and they went in. Chip gagged as he was hit with hot air that smelled like a toilet that hadn't been flushed in a year.

"Smells good!" Harvey cried.

Perhaps a hundred two-faced monkeys shot about the room in seeming madness, like raindrops in a hurricane. They bounced off walls, swung about from bars in the ceiling and the abundant furniture, and chittered so loudly Chip had to cover his ears.

"Ambassador Mok, where are you?" Colonel Muhammad asked. A dozen monkeys gathered about, chittering away as they rocked back and forth. She held out a portable translator.

"I'm Ambassador Mok!" cried one.

"No, I'm Ambassador Mok!" cried another.

"Don't believe them, I'm Ambassador Mok," cried still another. Soon dozens were claiming to be the ambassador.

"I gave a bead necklace to the real ambassador," said Colonel Muhammad. "Who has it?"

Several dozen held out their paws, each holding a bead.

"Damn it, I can't tell them apart!" Colonel Muhammad exclaimed. It was the first time Chip had seen her lose her cool.

"I'm Ambassador Mok!" another cried, jumping up and down. "Don't you recognize me?"

"No, no, it's me!"

"No me! I want to be the ambassador!" It tried to pull off the colonel's veil. She threw it and several others aside, but they kept coming, all insisting they were the ambassador. One jumped on Chip's head, reached down, and, upside down, began licking his face as he warded off other two-faced monkeys with his hands.

189

"*Enough!*" roared the colonel. "We're done here." She returned to the main office. Chip followed, with Harvey on his shoulder.

"That smell was worse than Ambassador Terror," Chip said. He was sure that nothing else could possibly ever smell bad to him again after experiencing that.

"May I be Ambassador Mok?" asked Harvey. Other than his red cap and translating device, he too looked identical to the others.

"*No!*" cried the colonel. Then she brightened. "Actually, why not? We need one. As of now, you are Ambassador Harvey, the representative of your people."

"Yay!"

"Okay, ambassador," Chip said. "Just one question: you seem to like people, so why do the Carmalite monkeys want to leave?"

"That obvious," said Harvey. "We like people, but people like put us in cages. We like trees, not cages."

Colonel Muhammad turned to Chip. "Your orders and detailed instructions have been sent to you. You have been assigned the *Wanderer*, a class five four-man starship explorer with cloaking capabilities. You leave at the end of the week."

"When do I meet the other members of the crew, the other members of the Resettlement Squad?"

Chip couldn't see her mouth, but he could just barely read the smile in her mind. "You already have. It was just Sergeant Juskers and me, now it's you and me, but I'm not going. In fact, as soon as you finish your mission, I'm transferring out. This isn't the most popular of assignments, trying to find home-worlds for rebelling pets. This is the military where we have other ways of putting down rebellions, and if you fail in your mission, I plan on leading the other method." She glanced down at her scaled gloves. "I liked that finger."

"But you said it was a four-man explorer!"

"Yes, adjusted for your three passengers. You and the three ambassadors. Good luck."

SEVEN

Chip had always wanted a family. Now he had one, with all the problems of your typical family—squabbling, fighting, and murder attempts. His only respite was to hide in his room reading and drinking coffee until the ship's computer or loud screams alerted him that he was needed. Each of the ambassadors also had their own quarters.

Ambassador Doby's salty aquarium was jammed into one. It had a portal on one side that allowed her to slide down into a wheeled water buggy. Once inside, Doby could drive it about the ship, guiding the steering wheel in the back with her flukes, and controlling the speed with a lever she grasped with one of her flippers. The tips of her flippers were surprisingly dexterous—one time Chip watched as the whale did adjustments to the buggy with a screwdriver and pliers grasped with the tips.

Ambassador Terror's room was kept perpetually cool. On day one, the walls were plain white. By day two she had painstakingly gone over her space with a black marker in her jaws, painting it entirely black. By day three she had drawn with a white marker dozens of pictures of snakes swallowing people, monkeys, and whales.

Ambassador Harvey's room was kept warm and moist, with bars in the ceiling and various furniture whose primary use was to launch him about the room. He slept in a human-sized bed overrun with stuffed animals of nearly every kind—with large snakes a major omission in the collection.

"Captain Brown, you are needed in Ambassador Doby's quarters," said the ship's computer the first morning out in its dull, monotone voice. He heard a deep scream of fright and the sound of breaking glass. He fell back into bed.

"Computer, I'm tired of calling you Computer," said Chip. "For now on I am going to call you…Jenny."

"Thank you, Captain Brown," said Jenny. "You are very much needed in Ambassador Doby's quarters."

"Please, call me Captain Chip," he instructed Jenny.

"Yes, Captain Chip," said Jenny. "You are *extremely* needed in Ambassador Doby's quarters."

Sighing, Chip got up and walked to the whale's room. Ambassador Terror was rearing up over the aquarium, jaws wide, the glass lid shattered on the floor. Apparently someone had never heard of plastic. The dwarf whale was at the bottom of the aquarium, her jaws wide in a rather non-threatening way since they were full of baleen, while the snake's mouth was full of teeth.

"Stop it!" Chip said, pulling out the handy taser he'd borrowed from Colonel Mohammad.

"I think I can fit it inthide me," said the giant snake, eyeing the whale.

"Stay out of my water!" cried the whale.

"Only one way to find out," continued Terror. She lunged forward into the water with breathtaking speed, jaws wide, and swallowed up the front fourth of the whale.

"Let go!" Chip yelled. Mumbling sounds came from Doby, who thrashed about in the water. Terror only swallowed more, now taking up the front third of the whale. Chip shot the taser. Immediately there were two screams, from the whale and the snake. The latter pulled back, practically spitting out the whale. Chip turned off the taser.

"Next time you do anything like that," Chip said, "and I might forget to turn off the taser. Now listen closely. Jenny— that's the computer's name, for those of you who didn't get the memo—do you recognize my voice?"

"Yes. You are Captain Forrest Brown, who I am to call Captain Chip."

"And who is the captain of this ship?"

"You are."

"Who gives the orders around here?"

"You do."

"I give orderth too!" said Terror.

"No you don't!" cried the whale.

"Do to!" Terror made a sudden move toward the whale, causing Doby to flinch and squeeze into the far corner of her tank.

"Ship, under no circumstances are you to take orders from any voice other than mine," Chip said. "Do you understand?"

"I understand," said Jenny.

"Now, Mr. Terror—"

"Ambathador Terror to you."

"Okay, 'Ambathador Terror', consider this. If you kill me, no one else can operate this ship, and we will all die."

"Then I can kill the otherth?"

"And if you kill Doby or Harvey, I will kill you, slowly and painfully." Chip held up the taser. "Wanna try me?"

"Tho no killing?"

"Exactly."

"Yay!" cried Harvey, jumping on Chip's shoulder and smothering him with kisses.

That afternoon, after Terror tried to catch Harvey with the excuse that she was only going to eat his legs, not kill him, they went through the whole rulebook again, this time making Terror promise not to kill, injure, hurt, stalk, scare, or even look funny at the others. She was also ordered to stay out of her fellow ambassadors' rooms.

This worked fine until there were more screams from the whale's room. This time Harvey was sitting in the corner, crying with both faces.

"I'm sorry, so sorry!" Doby said as Chip entered. "If I'd been able to kill you with one clean swat, you wouldn't be in such pain. I'm so, so sorry! I won't miss again!" It turned out Harvey had entered the whale's quarters and shot about the room, teasing Doby, who didn't understand the concept. He'd gotten too close to the tank, and as he sailed by, Doby had nailed him with a tail swat. Once again Chip had to lay down the law.

"If you promise to keep them both away from me," said Doby, "I promise not to look for ways to destroy the ship and kill us all. Terror broke my lid, and now I have no protection!"

"If you destroy the ship," Chip pointed out, "you'll die too."

"Sorry."

So Chip ordered Harvey to stay out of both ambassadors' rooms.

"Awww!" was his response, pouting with his sad face. "I just want to play."

"You want to play with this?" Chip asked, holding up the taser.

"No! I'll stay out." He gave Chip a big grin with his happy face.

"Done," Chip said, turning to the whale.

"Thank you," said Doby. "To show my great gratitude for your hospitality, the short-circuit bomb mechanism I planted is under the helm controls, set to go off in ten minutes."

Chip pretty much sprinted to the helm controls, and found the device. As he examined it, Doby entered on her water buggy.

"What the hell did you do?" Chip cried.

"With great apologies, I already told you, I planted the bomb under the helm controls, set to go off in—"

"I know, I know! But why?"

"Why? Because Ambassador Terror attacked me, and I couldn't bear her existing while I existed. But now I am so sorry, and if you cut the red wire, all will be well."

Chip didn't exactly trust Doby, so he examined the wiring, and verified that the red one was the wire to cut. Or at least he was pretty sure—there were also black and yellow wires. He waited until there were ten seconds left before he took a deep breath, and with a pair of wire cutters, cut the red wire.

The ship did not blow up in a fiery explosion. But Chip confined Doby to her quarters for the duration, and Terror as well just to be safe. He allowed them out for a common meal in the bridge once a day, where the three mostly glared at each other. After a few days, Terror and Doby chose to stay in their quarters, so Chip only saw them when delivering meals to their rooms, a job that fell to him by default.

So for the rest of the trip it was just him and Harvey spending their days together on the bridge. Which was fun until you realized spending weeks alone with a playfully hyperactive two-faced monkey was like being locked in a room with a five-year-old, with no letup. With Harvey sometimes excitedly talking with his front mouth and simultaneously chittering away with his back face—which Chip found rather disconcerting—it was like five-year-old Siamese twins. Fortunately Harvey slept about twelve hours out of each twenty-four-hour day, so after subtracting Chip's own eight hours, that left four hours of quiet, which he mostly spent reading, drinking coffee, and nibbling on banana nut muffins, his favorite.

Meals popped out of a chute three times a day, created by the computer. Chip ordered a variety of buffet dinners—the computer was surprisingly good—and non-stop coffee. Doby received a bucket of wiggling krill, two-inch long crustaceans. Terror received one live rat each day. Harvey received a variety of fruit. The first time the food came out of the chute Harvey grabbed his bowl of fruit, a handful of krill, and with his prehensile tail the rat, and ran for his room. The krill, out of water, quickly died, but the rat became his pet. Chip ordered the computer to deliver another rat, and so both ambassadors were fed—though Doby complained that there was slightly less krill than expected, and apologized for considering smashing Chip into a wall with her water buggy if this ever happened again.

The journey, mostly taken up traveling between wormholes, took two weeks. Chip's main joy on the trip was forgetting to warn Terror about the wormholes and listening to her surprised screams as they entered them. He also spent a lot of time with Harvey, playing games with his pet rat—which Harvey named "Rat"—and learning the Carmalite language. Soon he could chitter, whistle, and grunt the language well enough to have real conversations with Harvey, though the monkey's laughter at his apparent accent and poor pronunciation made communication difficult. Chip never did figure out how one could have an accent when whistling.

During his week on Earth he had studied the possible worlds for Carmalite monkeys, dwarf blue whales, and cottlesnakes. The number of habitable worlds in the galaxy far outnumbered those that had been surveyed, and those that had been surveyed far outnumbered those that had been occupied. Add in the complications of finding a convenient wormhole route to each star system while trying to figure out the requirements for each species, and it had been a long week.

He had decided on a surveyed planet currently known only as 382,567-C as their first stop. The planet had been claimed by the Terran Confederation, with an appropriate marker left behind, which presumably said, "Property of Terran Confederation." The planet was an easy pick, with 95% Earth gravity, a nitrogen-oxygen atmosphere (73%–26%), large saltwater oceans for dwarf blue whales, cool forests in the northern and southern regions for cottlesnakes, and warm jungles around the equator for Carmalite monkeys. The life on the planet was DNA based, compatible for Earth stomachs. Soon they were orbiting the planet, using the ship's cloaking device to keep it hidden from possible attackers.

However, assuming the planet worked out, which species would settle there? They'd learned on Earth the dangers of multiple intelligent species cohabiting together, so the plan was to find one planet for each. This first planet seemed perfect for all three, which is why he'd chosen it first. It seemed a dead ringer for Earth, except all the continents were wrong. There were three great oceans, with three continental masses separating them, plus lots of islands.

But first he had to verify what the original survey had tentatively found, that it was uninhabited by sentient beings.

There were three steps to follow for this: first, radio the planet and see if anyone answers. Second, take atmospheric and water samples and see if there are traces of technological waste, which could take days. Third, fly about the planet on full sensors and look for signs of intelligent beings, which could take days.

But first thing's first. "Jenny, prepare a worldwide radio broadcast."

"Done."

"Send the following message out in every known language, one after the other, in order of galactic usage." Then, speaking in Terran, he said, "Anyone here?" He waited for five minutes, tossing a ball against a wall as Harvey ran and grabbed it and brought it back, jumping up and down in excitement. The monkey had seven ways of grabbing the ball, and used them all—all four arms and legs, his tail, and both mouths.

"So much for step one," Chip said. "Jenny, take atmospheric samples for testing, and plan out where to land for water samples."

A few hours later they landed on a coastal area beside the largest of the three oceans, midway between the northern and equatorial areas. An almost earthlike jungle paralleled it for a thousand miles. Atmospheric tests had shown no signs of intelligent life, i.e. no contaminations—just pure air. Water tests would soon show the same thing. But there was an even more important test than the air and water tests.

All three ambassadors left to explore. Within minutes Doby was frolicking in the ocean, Terror was slithering about in the jungle, and Harvey was swinging from tree to tree, which looked almost earthlike—photosynthesis leads to green leaves no matter what the planet. Chip saw a few scurrying animals and some tiny buzzing insects. The salty air reminded him of Doby's quarters.

382,567-C had passed the ambassador test. Which led to a problem.

"I hereby claim this planet as the new world for dwarf blue whales," said Doby.

"Not a chanth," said Terror. "Thith ith our world, and we will thwallow any who dare oppothe uth. We'll move a bit north—too hot here."

"This world is for the Carmalite monkeys!" cried Harvey. "We'll just move a bit south to the warmer areas."

The simple solution, of course, would be for all three to settle this perfect world together, with blue whales in the oceans, cottlesnakes in the north and south, and Carmalite monkeys sandwiched in between—not a promising metaphor for the monkeys. Chip knew they needed separate worlds to settle. But who would get this first one?

He could commission a scholarly study that would look at all factors, creating a table showing the pluses and minuses for each respective species, and tabulate the results with a scientifically derived scoring system.

Or they could flip coins.

Since there were three of them, they would each toss a coin. If all three were heads or tails, then they would go again until there was an odd one out. The odd one out was the winner. They all met on the sand next to the ocean for the flipping, with Doby in her water buggy.

The blue whale went first. She balanced her body on her flukes so that her head and upper body were out of the water buggy, and flipped the coin with one of her flippers. Staring down at the coin in the sand, she cried, "It's heads!" She turned to the others. "You two need to roll tails so that we can begin the colonization of our new planet, which I hereby christen Whaleworld. You will have to leave or die. Sorry."

"Thnakeworld ith ourth," said Terror. "I mutht roll a tailth." She held up her own prominent tail, shaking the rattle on the end.

"Are you going to call it Thnakeworld or Snakeworld?" Chip asked, trying to ignore the creepy rattling. Some vestige of ancestral memory sent chills down Chip's spine.

"*Thnakeworld!*" cried Terror. She flipped the coin with her forked tongue. "*Yeth!*" she cried when it came up tails.

Harvey stared at Chip with the sad face on the back of his head. "We can't win!" he whimpered. "Heads it's snakes, tails it's whales. No Monkeyworld!"

The unhappy monkey slammed the coin into the ground, where it bounced about before coming to a stop—tails. Whaleworld it was.

"I am so sorry," Doby said to Terror. Then she looked up. "Yes!"

"We will thettle our own Thnakeworld thomewhere," said Terror. "We will make it the greatetht world, and then we will return here and take what a coin and you bumbling foolth hath taken from uth. All who oppothe uth will die."

They returned to the ship and prepared to take off. Doby would have liked to stay, but had to leave with them so she could return to Earth and lead her fellow whales to their new planet.

"One down, two to go!" Chip said. Things were going well.

"Captain Chip, there is an incoming message," said Jenny.

"That's not possible," Chip said. "We're alone out here. Aren't we?"

"No, we are not," said Jenny. "Here is the message."

"Hey, whoever you are, just got your message. Welcome to my planet! Hope you enjoy your brief stay!"

EIGHT

"Jenny, get the coordinates for whoever sent that message, and take us there," Chip said.

"The message had the coordinates attached and a text message," Jenny said. "It says, 'You are cordially invited to dinner tonight at seven p.m. in the great sovereign country of Novera here on the planet Noveraworld. Looking forward to dining with you!' It's signed Novera the Romera."

"You must reply to them," said Doby, "and apologize and explain that this planet is ours, and is called Whaleworld."

"Maybe you can do that personally," said Chip. "Seven p.m. is in half an hour. Any idea who Novera the Romera is?"

"There is a Torqual known as Novera the Romera," Jenny said. "In their language that means Novera the Laughing Killing Machine. He is the thirty-two–time Torqualian heavyweight free-fighting champion, who recently retired undefeated, and is now reported missing."

"And we found him!" Harvey exclaimed. "Maybe we get medals?"

Chip stuck a burner in his pocket, just in case things got interesting. Half an hour later they landed in the country of Novera. Which, it turned out, consisted of a campsite with a tent and a small scoutship, on a beach a few dozen feet from the ocean on one side, a jungle on the other.

Squatting in front of a campfire was the Torqual. He rose to greet them: nine feet tall, biped, purple-skinned, with a nose on each side of his head, and a blank spot between his eyes and mouth where a human nose would be. He wasn't just tall; he was husky, a thousand pounds of sheer bulging muscles coming out of places where Chip didn't have places. His inordinately long arms nearly reached the ground, with biceps and fists the size of Chip's head. He was dressed in some sort of black and white striped furry animal skin wrap, with a knife and huge burner on his belt.

"Welcome to the country of Novera!" said the towering Torqual as they came out of their ship, with Doby in her water buggy. He had a rather silly-looking grin on his face and a translator attached to a rope around his neck. "I am Novera." He extended a hand toward Chip. "Shaking hands is a human tradition, correct?" Unable to actually grasp the giant's hand in his, Chip resorted clasping his hand with one of Novera's fingers—he had six of them, plus two opposing thumbs. He similarly shook hands—or at least a finger—with Harvey, and with Doby's flipper. Terror surprised Chip by extending her tail to the alien, and Novera grabbed her rattle and gave it an affectionate shake.

"My name is—" Chip began.

"You are Forrest 'Chip' Brown," said Novera. "Captain of the *Wanderer*. Your passengers are Doby, Terror, and Harvey. I read all about you on the *Galactic News*."

"So you know why we are here?"

"Of course. And I have some great leads for you after you've left my planet."

"We'll talk about that—"

"After we've eaten. I've researched all four of your species, and found a perfect food to synthesize for dinner, something we can all enjoy." He held out a wooden branch he'd apparently cut from a local tree. At the end of it was a brown tubular object, about six inches long. "This is called a hot dog."

"We're eating dog?" asked Terror, shaking his rattle in apparent excitement.

"Better," said Novera. "I've gathered sticks for each of you. You put the stick through the hot dogs, which were created by my ship's food synthesizer from local animal life, and hold it over the fire to cook it. Then you stick it in a piece of bread, put various condiments on it, and eat it. Like this. I already cooked this one." He reached into a basket by the fire and pulled out a bread roll with a slit cut in it, and put the hot dog in the slit. Next to the basket were five small bowls, each with a different colored sauce—red, yellow, orange, green, and blue. Novera spooned a little of each onto the hot dog, and then took a big bite. "Delicious!"

Terror was the first to join in. She wrapped her tail around a stick, then wrapped the tip of her tail around a hot dog, and jammed it onto the tip of the stick. The other three quickly followed. Soon the five different species all sat in their various ways around the fire, roasting hot dogs.

"It's great having temporary visitors!" Novera said. "Maybe I'll cook something called an omelet for your breakfast before you all leave in the morning!"

"About that," Chip said. "Didn't you see the *Property of Terran Confederation* marker? It has an automatic radio beacon to alert everyone that the planet has been claimed."

"Oh that," said Novera, laughing. "First thing I did when I arrived was dismantle it and throw it into the ocean. After all, after they claimed the planet, they abandoned it, and so the claim is no longer valid. I've put in my own claim. This is now my retirement world, and it's all mine." He pointed at a nearby tree, which had something carved into it in a foreign language. "It says, *This planet property of Novera the Romera.* And just think, there are perhaps millions of planets like this all over the galaxy where you can make your own claims!"

"This planet is now Whaleworld," said Doby. "Terran Confederation legally claimed it, and now it belongs to the dwarf blue whales. I'm so sorry to have to tell you this."

Novera threw back his head and laughed, his two noses shaking back and forth. He reached out and patted the top of the whale's head. "I've already explained that their claim is no longer valid." He tapped the translator device on his neck twice with a huge finger. "Silly translator must be defective."

"I apologize for my poor communication skills," said Doby. "Whaleworld is ours."

"I couldn't agree more!" Novera exclaimed. "And I will fight to the death for your right to colonize that planet, wherever in the galaxy it might be."

"I think we have a misunderstanding here," Chip interjected, quietly moving his hand toward the hidden burner.

"There is no misunderstanding," said Novera, suddenly no longer smiling. "The Terrans claimed this planet, then abandoned it. I then claimed it, and did not abandon it. Now you want to take what is mine away from me, and you," and he pointed at Chip, "are now reaching for your burner. I wouldn't." He held up his other hand, where he held his much larger burner.

"Maybe you could share the planet?" asked Harvey. Novera looked down on the tiny monkey, who was squatting down next to him, and once again he was smiling. Harvey's front face faced the alien; the sad one faced Chip, and it looked terrified.

"I don't share," Novera said. He gently patted Harvey on the head.

"Thith ith delithiouth!" cried Terror, pulling the stick from her mouth, which she still held with her tail. She grabbed another hot dog and began roasting it on her stick.

Chip slowly pulled his hand away from his pocketed burner, and instead pulled his own hot dog out from over the fire. Unlike Terror, who had eaten it plain, he wrapped his in bread, covered it with all five gooey sauces, and took a bite.

"It is good!" he said. He motioned at Harvey and Doby, who both were very still, holding their hot dogs over the fire. They removed theirs, and soon all five were enjoying the hot dogs.

"They are better than rat," said Terror.

"Better than krill," said Doby.

"Better than fruit!" cried Harvey.

"Then I hereby declare today's culinary adventures and this multi-species meeting a smashing success," said Novera, the burner now on his lap. He was once again smiling. "Now, would you like to leave now, or in the morning?"

"Sorry, but there are four of us and only one of you," said Doby. "You can only get one of us before the rest of us get you. I am so sorry."

Novera's arm flashed, and in a split second four beams shot out so rapidly they seemed to come out all at once. Four hot dogs that had been roasting over the fire were suddenly well done. "I believe your hot dogs are ready," said Novera.

"So you claim this planet by waving a burner at us?" asked Chip.

"You reached for yours first. Would you prefer to fight me for it, four on one?"

Chip studied the smiling giant squatting by the fire. He'd had plenty of hand-to-hand training in the military, and knew how to fight against bigger, presumably slower opponents. But he'd just seen how fast Novera was; no human could have matched that firing speed, and no doubt he was equally fast in hand-to-hand combat. Jenny had said that Novera was the many-time champion of his planet in some fighting discipline. No, he realized, he didn't stand a chance against the alien.

But four on one? He glanced over at Terror. She was built for fighting, though not in the conventional sense. And he knew how fast Doby was with her flukes, which carried a wallop—but would she be of much use in a real fight, rolling about in a water buggy? And Harvey—what good was he in a fight?

"Letth fight!" cried Terror, rattling her tail. But Doby didn't look so sure, and Harvey, who had sat next to the giant, had slowly moved to the far side of the fire and cowered in the background.

"Come at me, large snake," said Novera. "Since you have no arms, I too will not use my arms." He put his arms behind his back and walked out along the beach a dozen feet from the fire.

Terror slowly slithered her way toward the alien. Chip had seen how fast she could strike, and wondered if her poison would affect the alien. Without his arms, what chance would the Torqual have?

The two slowly circled each other. "I will thwallow you," said Terror, fanning out her neck, her head bobbing up and down hypnotically. Chip couldn't help but chuckle—that would be something to see, Terror trying to swallow the huge alien.

"And I will thwottle you," said Novera.

"Are you mocking me?"

"Yeth," Novera said, laughing. "Oh, and I always research my opponents. That's why I've *never* lost a fight. That cobra poison you have—it won't affect me."

Chip wished he could replay what happened next in slow motion because it happened so fast it was like watching a flash of lightning. As near as he could tell, Terror struck at Novera, jaws wide, fangs extended, seemingly a flashing whip moving at the speed of sound. But just as thunder cannot outrace lightning, there was an even faster flash as Novera leaped forward, thrust his head down, and grabbed Terror's tail in his mouth. Then things slowed down as the alien stood upright, swinging the fifteen-foot thrashing snake in a circle once, twice, and then, on the third circuit, flung her hundreds of feet out to sea. There was a distant splash.

"Who's next?" asked Novera, the silly grin on his face clashing with the flashing eyes above. His arms, no longer behind his back, bulged with muscles. "Or all three at once? Or four, if your snake survived and swims back? What's it going to be, fight or flight?"

"We should go!" cried Harvey. Chip thought this made perfect sense. So did Doby; she was already rolling toward the ship.

Chip stared out at the ocean where Terror had disappeared. And then saw a small splash, as Terror surfaced. They watched as the snake swum back to shore with a side-to-side undulating stroke.

"Round two!" cried the snake as she emerged, slither-charging at Novera.

"No!" said Doby. She'd stopped moving toward their ship, and had intersected Terror's path, blocking her with her water buggy. "We leave and find another planet. Otherwise we die here. I'm sorry."

Terror raised her head to full eye level with the nine-foot Torqual. She stuck her forked tongue in and out several times as she stared at the alien. Then she said, "I will return thomeday and eat you." Then she turned and slivered toward the ship.

Chip also stared at the alien. "What if we return and attack from the air with our ship?"

"Your ship's a class five starship explorer armed with a burner that might not get through my tent walls. My scoutship's got a mega-burner that would blow you out of the sky with a single burst. I could probably punch through your ship's armor with my fist. You could go back to the Resettlement Squad and ask for a better ship…except I heard that they are disbanding, and that after you return there will be no more resettlement plans for the emerging intelligent races on your planet."

"How the hell are you getting all this news?" Chip asked.

"As I said, I subscribe to the *Galactic News*," Novera said. "I pay for a direct channel. What, your agency doesn't pay for that, and so you are out here, all alone and out of contact with your boss? Between that and my better ship, I'm guessing I have more money than your Resettlement Squad." He clapped his hands together three times. "You've done great, and I admire you, and if you ever want to have a round two, come on back. Or perhaps after you've found other planets to settle your pets, stop by to visit and we'll have dinner again. Oh, and I'll take this."

With a sudden movement of unbelievable speed, Novera grabbed Chip with one giant hand around his neck. Then the alien casually pulled Chip's burner from his pocket. He released Chip, and held out Chip's burner in his hand. He closed his fist, grimaced for a moment, and then opened it. There was little left of Chip's burner other than a bit of misshapen metal. The alien dropped it at Chip's feet.

Enough was enough; Chip lashed out at the alien. His years of training in hand-to-hand fighting meant that he reflexively knew that the way to fight an opponent with much longer reach was to get inside their defense and punch away. Only—there was no getting through the alien's arms, which blocked his path no matter how much he swerved and veered. And then, as the alien laughed, Novera dropped his arms. Instantly Chip was inside, pounding away at the alien's body.

It was like punching a tree. There was no effect on the alien. Chip tried punching the face, but now the alien dodged, and Chip was unable to land a blow on the swerving head. Then he went low—perhaps the alien had the same between-the-legs weakness of human males. But apparently not as Novera only laughed.

Under stress, Chip suddenly could read the laughter in Novera's mind, which only angered him. He lashed out mentally, visualizing his mind as a giant fist of light plowing into Novera's brain like a meteor. But it just bounced off.

"Mental powers?" asked Novera. "I'm impressed. But of course I've trained against far stronger telepaths. I wouldn't be undefeated if any minor telepath like yourself could take me down. So…anymore tricks?"

Chip tried punching again, pumping both fists as fast as he could. Novera easily brushed his attempts aside with one long arm, and reached out and patted Chip on the head with the other.

"Now it is my turn," said Novera. He suddenly grabbed both of Chip's arms in one giant fist and lifted him into the air. Then, with Chip helplessly dangling from the alien's grip, Novera patted him in the face with his other hand.

"You are my guests," said Novera, still patting him playfully. "So I won't kill you this time." Then the alien gave his nose a squeeze. "Only one, how pitiful." Then he suddenly opened his fist. Chip fell to the ground, tumbling off his feet.

"Next time it will be to the death. Now leave my planet!"

Chip rose to his feet, breathing heavily. There was no way of defeating the alien. But the news was far worse than that. The Resettlement Squad closed? So much for the great enlightened human race, finding homes for their former pets. And now this planet, so perfect for them, was out of reach. The future of an entire race changed because of the doings of one big bully? This couldn't stand. And yet…there was nothing they could do. He turned abruptly and walked back to the ship.

"Don't forget your hot dogs!" cried Novera, holding out the picnic basket. But they were already boarding their ship, and quickly took off.

NINE

"That was embarrassing," said Chip. They were on their way to the next planet on their list, 227,129-D. It was another earthlike planet, another seeming Eden like the previous planet, also claimed by the Terran Confederation. Chip had eased the restrictions on the ambassadors, and all four of them crowded in the bridge.

"You are all cowardth," said Terror.

"We are all alive!" said Harvey.

"You are not alive," said Terror. "You merely ecthitht."

"And someday you will exist on a planet of your own, with all your fellow serpents," said Doby. "Then you can take turns eating each other."

"And apologizing for it, right?" asked Harvey.

Doby looked at the monkey. "Sorry?" She sounded confused.

Soon they were orbiting the planet, hidden behind the ship's cloaking device. Once again they radioed to see if there were any current occupants. There seemingly were none. Chip had Jenny test the air, and it was breathable. Soon they were on the planet's surface, on a beach similar to the one they had recently left.

"Let me go for a swim," said Doby.

"I go swimming, too!" Harvey said. He raced ahead of Doby and stepped in the water—and screamed. He was quickly out of the water, his feet badly burned. The planet's oceans were acidic.

The next planet they surveyed was 157,251-B. It had a developing indigenous lifeform, essentially sentient walking cactuses.

Next up was 376,713-C. In the time since the initial survey of the planet someone had decided it would be a good testing ground for nuclear-type weapons. The planet's surface was radioactive and burned to a crisp. Chip shuddered at the thought of these weapons.

"This is crazy!" cried Doby six months later. They had surveyed 23 systems to no avail. "We had a planet for my race, and now, because of one creature, we have none."

"Even if we had that planet, we'd still need two more," said Chip. "We can't return to Earth until then or they'll take our ship away since there will be no more Resettlement Squad."

"What ith point?" asked Terror. "If we find planet, who will thend our people to rethettle them? Humanth have given up on uth."

"They've stopped actively looking for planets to resettle your races," said Chip, "but if we find three planets to send your races to, I think Earth'll be happy to be rid of the problem. Exporting is less costly than policing."

"Wouldn't it be simpler to find one planet?" asked Harvey. "One planet, three races?"

"History tells us that doesn't work very well," Chip said. "When two races meet, one always ends up taking over the other."

"When two races meet," said Harvey. "When wild animals meet in jungle, they fight. But when wild animals grow up together, they become like a family. Our races would grow up together."

"The little monkey might have something," said Doby. "On Earth, humans already had settled the planet, so we never had a chance. But if we settle it together, we'd be equals. Plus, we'd be in the ocean, the monkeys would be on land." There was a silence as all but one was thinking the same thing.

"Why ith everyone looking at me?" asked Terror.

"I think whales and monkeys might be able to share a planet—I'm not sure—but I'm not so sure about snakes," said Chip.

"Big snakes, little monkeys—I'm scared!" said Harvey.

Terror reared up on her tail so that she was looking down on all of them. "You don't underthtand cottlethnaketh. You think we're jutht bruteth, alwayth trying to eat otherth. You jutht don't underthtand."

"We're so sorry," said Doby. "What don't we understand?"

"Yeah, always wanting to eat others seems an accurate assessment," said Chip.

"Like us!" said Harvey.

Terror looked side to side, her forked tongue shooting in and out a few times. "We do want to eat otherth. But only becauthe they are *otherth*. Don't you thee?"

"See what?" asked Chip.

"I get it," said Doby. "You eat others. If we were not others, but instead were like family to you, growing up together, then we wouldn't be others, and you'd be on our side."

"We'll be brothers, not others!" cried Harvey.

Terror nodded her head. "You are either with uth, or not with uth. If you are with uth, then we are intenthly loyal. If you are otherth, then we eat you."

"And what are we now?" asked Doby.

"Now?" Terror stuck her tongue for a long second, then drew it back in. "You are otherth."

"I guess that answers our question," said Chip. "We need to find at least two suitable worlds."

"No," said Doby. "We may be others now, but we can *become* brothers and sisters. We have to earn it from Terror, but our descendants would grow up with them, and *be* brothers and sisters to them."

"I think you're all a bit naïve about this," said Chip.

"Would you rather wander the galaxy looking for worlds, or let us learn to get along on one world?"

"We don't even have one world!" Chip yelled, slamming his fist against the wall and leaving a dent. "We had one, and we were run off like a bunch of mice!" He punched the wall two more times, one for each ambassador. The respective ambassadors stared, never having seen him so lose his temper.

"There ith one tholution," said Terror.

"Yes," said Doby. "Very sorry."

The snake and whale both looked down at the monkey, who was breathing rapidly and watching them with wide, frightened eyes on both faces.

"I don't know," said Chip.

Harvey turned around, and faced them with his front face. His lip trembled, but he no longer looked terrified, merely stoic. "Yes," he said.

"Then we go back and fight the Torqual for our world," said Doby. "*Our* world."

"Our world," said Harvey and Terror together.

And so the decision was made.

TEN

"We will call our world Swem," said Harvey. They were about to enter the final wormhole that would take them back to what had originally been 382,567-C, then Whaleworld, and was now Noveraworld.

"Why Swem?" Chip asked.

"I discussed with others," said Harvey. "S for snake. W for whale. M for monkey. Swem!"

"What about the E?"

"E for everybody!" said the monkey, spinning about energetically and smiling from both faces. "We invite everybody as guests. But Terror disagree, says it's for Eat, as in eating those who are not snake, whale, or monkey. Whale wanted to call world Swam, Swim, or Swum, but that silly. She agreed to Swem because she just wants to eat krill and hot dogs."

"Sorry, I wasn't able to get the synthesizer to make hot dogs."

"We'll get recipe from Novera."

It was time to enter the wormhole. This time Chip alerted them all, including Terror, and so they were ready for the usual stomach flip flops. Soon they were orbiting what they hoped to rename Swem.

They were not stupid; they knew what they were up against. The Torqual was the greatest fighter in his race's history. He was stronger and faster than any of them, and had fighting skills far beyond theirs. What chance did they have?

And yet Chip couldn't help but think that in a battle of four on one, the four, if they organized properly, should win. It was just a matter of planning, training, and discipline. And hope. Lots of hope. In fact, against this monster of a creature, mostly hope.

Only Chip and Terror were trained in fighting and had true fighting skills. Doby had great power in her thrashing tail, but little mobility in her water buggy, and baleen instead of teeth. And Harvey...was Harvey. The monkey was the only one who might match Torqual in sheer speed, but faced a roughly 50-1 size and 1000-1 ferocity-in-combat deficit.

They landed on the far side of the planet away from Novera's campsite, on a similar beach next to a jungle. And there, for three weeks, they practiced. Chip took the lead as the trained military person, and even Terror followed his instructions. But drilling the moves against an imaginary giant and actually fighting him were two very different things. There was no serious stand-in for Novera; all they could do was practice the moves they planned. They found an appropriate tree which, after they did some cutting, was nine feet tall with two protruding branches as "arms." They practiced against the unmoving tree, and if Novera would only stand as still as the tree as he fought, Chip knew they would win.

Chip wanted more time to whip his three ambassadors into shape, but soon it became apparent that there wasn't much more they could do. After three weeks they could do the moves flawlessly; another week, month, or year of practicing the moves wasn't going to make them much better.

At the start of the fourth week they landed at Novera's campsite in the country of Novera. The four of them approached Novera's perpetual fire like a funeral march. Novera was squatting by the fire, as if he hadn't left it since their departure. He rose to greet them with the usual huge smile.

"Welcome back, my little guests. Are you back for more hot dogs?" His huge burner hung conspicuously at his side.

"We are here to fight you for thith planet," said Terror.

"Really?" said the grinning Torqual. "You enjoy swimming?"

"Remember, you agreed to four on one," said Chip.

"Of course," said Novera. "Are you counting your little monkey as a full one?" Harvey turned his back on the alien, glaring at him with the face on the back of his head. "So let's get started. *To the death!* Should someone go *ding*, and we begin?" He moved out onto the beach away from the fire, and reached down and rubbed his hands in the sand to improve his grip. Chip did the same.

"Ding!" cried Doby from her water buggy in a ground-shaking cry that caused her own companions to hesitate as much as the alien. And then all four charged even as Novera, holding his ground in a slight crouch, roared with laughter. They stopped well outside of Novera's reach, then spread out, surrounding and circling him, clockwise, as Novera lightly bounced up and down on his feet, an amazing sight for a nine-foot, one-thousand pound being.

"Are we going to fight or are we going to dance?" asked Novera.

"Charge!" cried Chip. All four again charged at Novera. Harvey, easily the fastest, got there first, as planned—but only for a second as Novera nonchalantly smacked him away. The other three hesitated and came to a stop. Harvey hit the ground far away. He rolled to his feet, shaking his head, looking dazed.

"One little smack, and you all freeze up?" asked Novera. "I'm disappointed. You have to expect casualties in a battle such as this. You do understand what *to the death* means?" He turned to Harvey. "And you, little one. Did you learn anything from your charge?"

Harvey screamed something unintelligible, and suddenly raced off into the jungle.

"So much for your cowardly little friend," said Novera. "And now there are three. Shall we continue?"

They circled Novera for another moment. And then Chip cried out the pre-arranged signal, *"Together!"* Immediately Terror and Doby moved to him so they were all side-by-side, the jungle to their right, the ocean to their left, with Terror in the middle, flanked by Chip and Doby.

Novera stopped his light bouncing and stood up straight, hands on hips. *"No, No, NO!"* he cried. "You are doing this all wrong! You are making three fundamental errors." He held up a finger. "First, you are hanging back, waiting for me to attack. This allows me to take you out one at a time. Don't you realize how much faster I am than any of you? I can just lash out, like this." One of his long arms nonchalantly shot out, smacking Chip across the face so hard that quasars and supernovas circled his head. He went flying back onto the sand, the world swirling about in a dizzy panorama. Maybe, he thought, Harvey had the right idea. But they had to see this through. He quickly rose back to his feet and rejoined his companions.

"Second," continued Novera, holding up a second finger, "you have the sun behind me, so it's in your eyes. You should circle so that you have the sun in *my* eyes.

"And third," and he held up three fingers, "because all of you are all on one side of me, I can see and defend against all three of you with ease. You should surround me as you did before so you can come at me from three sides. I've spent many difficult years training for such attacks, and here you've wasted all that training by staying together and making this all too easy. Come on, let's make it at least somewhat competitive, shall we?"

"Closer!" cried Chip, and the three of them crowded even closer together. They circled to their left, so they were now between Novera and the ocean. They slowly advanced on Novera. *"Closer!"* he repeated, even louder.

"You just aren't getting the message," said Novera, shaking his head. "You now have the sun out of your eyes, but if you were smart, you'd have circled all the way around to put it in mine. And you've made a fourth error." He held up four fingers. "Your whole attack formation is wrong. You have your least mobile attacker, the fish in a water buggy, on the side. You should put her in the middle doing a frontal attack, with your two more mobile attackers on the side where they can try to flank me." He sighed, and held up a fifth finger. "And you've made a fifth error. You are now between me and the ocean. You should try to trap *me* against the ocean, as the water would slow me down, perhaps slightly equalizing things— maybe even letting your big fish there come out of his tank and really fight." He shook his head disdainfully, then held up a sixth finger. "Plus you've—"

That's when Harvey charged out of the jungle from behind Novera, landed on the back of his head, and put his hands over the alien's eyes.

"About time!" Chip grumbled as the three charged the alien. He grabbed one of Novera's arms and hung on for dear life. Doby leaped out of her water buggy, closed her baleen-filled mouth over Novera's other arm, and also hung on.

Terror went straight for the head, jaws wide, and before the blinded alien could react, had swallowed his head and neck. The alien thrashed about, but with Chip and Doby holding his arms, he wasn't able to dislodge the snake. Terror extended his jaws even more and pulled them over the alien's shoulders. Soon she had swallowed the alien all the way to the upper chest, her skin going so taut Chip worried it would tear and the struggling alien would explode out. Novera's two noses, one on each side of his head, forced the skin out even more on each side, like a pair of huge pimples.

How long could Novera go before he suffocated?

About ten minutes, or at least that's how long it took before the alien went still. No longer worried that Novera's powerful arms could rip her apart from inside, Terror began to swallow the rest of him, and quickly reached his waist, so all that was visible of the alien were his legs. Chip and Doby released Novera's arms as they began to disappear into the snake's mouth.

"Let him go," Chip said. Terror, unable to answer with her mouth and body full of alien, just looked at him.

"Are you crazy?" asked Doby. "He wakes up and we're all dead. He's not going to fall for that trick again. Sorry!"

"We're not killers," Chip said. Terror's eyes went wide. "We've won the fight. Novera's an honorable warrior and will accept that. Besides, he's probably dead. And if he isn't, and does wake up, I've got this." Using two hands, he held up Novera's giant burner.

Terror eyed Chip for a moment, and then seemed to droop. Slowly the snake pulled back, essentially spitting the alien out in slow motion, leaving him lying on the ground on his back. Doby undulated along the ground back to her water buggy, and then, with a powerful thrust from her tail flukes, pushed herself back into it.

"He taithted bad anyway," said Terror. "Like moldy mithe."

The alien began to stir. Chip covered him with the burner, keeping his distance just in case—he'd seen how fast and far Novera could lash out.

Then the alien's eyes popped open, and he smiled. "Wow. So this is what defeat tastes like, like bitter sand on the tongue. I've never had that taste before."

"Can't taithte worthe than moldy mithe," said Terror, slowly sticking her tongue in and out between tightened lips as if trying to remove the taste.

"Okay, you all win," said Novera. "I badly underestimated you. The planet is yours. I'll find another."

"Where ith Harvey?" Terror suddenly asked. They looked about, but the monkey was nowhere to be seen. There were no footprints on the sand leading to the jungle or the shore. He couldn't have left the scene. Then they all looked at Terror. Could it be?

"I mutht have thwallowed him!" the snake cried. She rolled onto her back, looking herself over.

"He was supposed to leap free when Terror attacked!" Chip said. "Like we practiced!"

"Wouldn't there be a bulge if you swallowed Harvey?" asked Doby.

"Not if thwallowed lengthwithe," said Terror. "He cannot thurvive inthide me long. You mutht cut me open."

"What?" Chip cried.

"I have a knife in my belt," said Novera, still lying on the ground. Sitting up, he offered it to Chip, who hesitated at first. Could it be a ploy? Would the alien stab him as he reached to take it? But he had to trust the alien now. He put the burner on the ground and accepted the knife.

He turned to Terror. "Are you sure about this?"

"We are team," said Terror. "I cannot thwallow a partner. I told you cottlethnaketh are loyal. Quickly now, before he dieth!"

Chip leaned in, hesitating, and then made a small incision in the middle of Terror's long belly. The snake jerked at the touch. Red blood seeped out.

"Fathter!" cried Terror.

Chip braced himself to make a longer, deeper cut. This might save Harvey, but he was about to murder his partner in a particularly painful and bloody way. This would have been easier at the start of their adventure, but now, Terror was as much a part of the team as any other. But what choice did he have? He took a deep breath, and prepared to cut deep along the snake's long body.

"Wait!" cried Novera. The alien rolled to his side. And there was Harvey, lying still, jammed into the sand where he'd been trapped beneath the alien.

"Ith he okay?" asked Terror.

"I don't think so," said Novera. "I think I crushed or suffocated him." He examined the monkey, and put his ear to his chest. "His heart has stopped. He is dead."

"I'm so sorry!" cried Doby.

"It ith my fault," said Terror. "I thought I had thwallowed him, and while we thought that, he wath thuffocating."

And so the monkey had met his end, right when they had succeeded in finding him and his kind a planet. What a dirty trick. Chip wanted to punch the universe.

Novera tapped him on the shoulder, and Chip spun about, fists up, ready to punch the alien in lieu of the universe. "My burner has a special taser setting," Novera said. "If I put it at full power, I might be able to revive him."

"Do it," Chip said, still balling his fists.

Novera scooped up his burner from the ground, and once again he had them at their mercy. Except…Chip felt something from the alien. A certain…goodness and honor. The alien could be trusted. Novera made an adjustment to his burner, setting it for taser. Then he held it against Harvey's chest.

"Everyone, back," Novera said. Then he fired the taser. Harvey jerked, then went still again. Novera put his head to Harvey's chest again, then shook his head. He gave a series of chest compressions, and then shocked the monkey again. Again Harvey jerked, but again went still, with Novera again listening for a heartbeat, and then doing more chest compressions. The alien did it a third time—and after putting his head to the monkey's chest once again, let out a loud shriek.

"His heart is beating!" They all gathered around, and a moment later Harvey opened his eyes, and looked about with both faces. He saw Novera leaning over him, screamed, and tried to get up, but stumbled.

Chip grabbed him. "Relax! Novera's on our side now. We won. The planet is ours."

"He lay on top of me!" the monkey cried. "I couldn't breathe!"

"And yet he's the one who saved you," Chip said. He turned to Novera. "Where'd you learn that?"

"Just an old trick from the fighting pits back home," he said. "And now it's time for me to pack and leave." He looked about forlornly. "It was to be my retirement world."

"If he saved me, then he stay with us," said Harvey. "Only him!" Then he frowned with both faces. "My head hurts!"

"You won the planet fair and square," said Novera.

"Do you have a wife or kids?" asked Chip.

"No, just me."

"Please don't mind me asking," said Doby, "but how old are you, and how long do Torquals live?"

"Assuming my translator gets this right, I'm 57, about one-third our normal lifespan."

"Then we should invite you to stay," said Doby. "Terror, you agree?"

"Yeth. He may have thith area ath long ath he live. Welcome to Thwem!"

ELEVEN

A few weeks later Chip was on Earth's moon, meeting with Colonel Muhammad. "Welcome back, Captain Forrest Brown. As you may know, the Resettlement Squad is closing down."

"But we found a planet where all three races could live," Chip said. "Wasn't that the plan?"

"The plan was three planets, one for each race. What do you think will happen when you put three intelligent races on one planet? Eventually there is only one."

"That's when you put a more developed race with a less developed one," said Chip. "These three races will develop together, as family, as brothers and sisters growing up together, with the snakes in the colder climates, the monkeys in the warmer ones, and the whales in the oceans."

She scoffed. "Snakes, monkeys, and whales? Brothers and sisters? Why don't we put snakes with rats, monkeys with fruit, and whales with krill? I'm sure they'd get along nicely."

"Their ambassadors have all agreed to this."

"They agreed to share a world with Terror and her kind? Are we talking about the same snakes?"

"Things changed during our trip. We learned a lot about each other. Cottlesnakes aren't evil, at least to their friends. They are fiercely loyal, and I think their descendants will honor what their ancestors forged, three races as one family."

She stared at him intently for a moment with her dark eyes peering out of her veil. Then she laughed. "Okay, have it your way. Or more precisely, you already had your way. Things have gotten much worse while you were away. A cottlesnake swallowed his owner just last week, blue whales keep finding ways to escape their tanks and blow up buildings, and Carmalite monkeys are almost impossible to handle now—they are rioting in the streets, and they're too fast to catch. We had funding to send them to three planets; sending them all to one planet will actually save money. All I can say is good riddance. Someday perhaps we will see what we have wrought."

"I can't wait to tell them the great news!"

"You'd better hurry," she said. "They leave for Earth tonight, where they'll be organizing the colonization of Swem. But you—you are still part of the Galactic Surveying Division."

"I joined the Resettlement Squad!"

"Which is part of the GSD. We're still doing resettlements; there are other emerging intelligent pets on Earth—those damn geneticists are headaches. Winged poodles, giant fire-breathing frogs, super squids that do quantum mechanics in their heads—what were they thinking? We'll need to find worlds for them all. And so you have a new assignment—you will be surveying worlds for possible terraforming and/or re-settlement. Welcome to your new assignment and your new title, Chief Surveyor Forrest Brown. Now go say goodbye to your friends before it's too late."

TWELVE

The three ambassadors were in a meeting when Chip barged in.

"Who the hell are you?" an elderly general exclaimed as Harvey, chittering from both mouths, leaped across the meeting table and into Chip's arms. Five other heavily decorated men and two scientific types also stared at Chip. On the wall next to the table was a huge star map, with a red circle around the Swem star system.

"I'm the guy who solved all your problems," Chip said. He opened his mouth to say more but a splash of water from Doby as she leaped from her water buggy by the table temporarily ended that. The whale reared up, balancing on her flukes, and gave him a crushing hug that threatened to squeeze all air from his lungs. Harvey climbed up and hugged his face, covering his nose. Then it got worse as Terror, slivering from the table like a torpedo, joined the huddle, throwing two coils around Chip's stomach and squeezing.

"Don't worry about ugly general," Terror said. "I eat him before we leave tonight."

"Oh, sorry," said Doby when Chip began to gag. "Maybe we should let him breathe?" She let go, and fell back on her belly on the floor. Harvey leaped off Chip's face and onto the whale's back. Terror loosened her grip, but didn't let go as she maneuvered her head directly in front of the gasping Chip.

"We and our kind will never forget you." She stuck out her forked tongue, tasting the air in front of Chip. "You will alwayth be welcome on Thwem. And I will alwayth remember your tathte, which I will dethcribe for otherth of my kind to alwayth remember."

"Thank you," Chip said between gulps for air. Then he threw his arms around Terror's neck. "I won't forget you either. None of you."

"This is all very sentimental," said the old general, "but we have to take these three to the infirmary now for some final meds before they leave tonight."

Terry slithered to the old general, and tasted the air in front of him. "I will alwayth remember your tathte ath well. For different reathonth. May I have you for dinner tonight?"

"Join *you* for dinner?" the general cried. "Not a chance!"

"That not ecthactly what I thaid. I will track you down before we leave." Terror turned back to Chip. "We leave thoon."

"It's horrible, but we'll probably never see each other again," said Doby. "I'm so sorry!"

"Come visit!" cried Harvey, once again jumping into Chip's arms. "We will build a monument to you!" And then there was a second group hug, which Chip barely survived. He barely remembered them finally disentangling, with Harvey grabbing hold of his hair and pulling out a few before he was finally pulled away. The old and possibly doomed general led the three ambassadors out, each waving back at Chip in their own way—Doby with her flukes out the back of her water buggy, Terror with her tail, and Harvey last, walking backwards and looking glum as he waved both hands.

And then they were gone. Once again he'd had a family, and once again he'd lost it.

THIRTEEN

His next assignment was to survey the 55 Cancri star system. Now he journeyed alone, still in the *Wanderer*. Having two people on a ship was "wasteful," as the ship and the surveying tools were mostly automated. He missed the excitement of Harvey racing and jumping about the bridge. Now the ambassador chambers were used as storage areas for the many samples he'd be bringing back.

The second, third, and fourth planets in the Cancri system were heavily populated by an intelligent race called the Cartheelis. But the fifth planet seemed uninhabited. So that's where he landed. The *Wanderer*'s cloaking device had been upgraded so he was confident the Cartheelis would not detect the ship. And then he went to work.

To truly judge a planet's viability, Chip was tasked with testing its air, water, and land. Air and water were easy; the ship did most of that. But for the land, he had to travel about the planet's surface, finding specimens for the ship to test.

He was so busy in his work he only vaguely noticed a shadow over him. He looked back, and that's when he saw the Cartheelis, a dozen of them, all staring at him as if he were the specimen. He very slowly finished bottling the mineral specimen in his hand, quickly scrawling a label, and put it in his bag. Then he slowly rose to meet the aliens. They were larger than humans, green, humanoid but with three legs. Like the

Torqual, they had six-fingered hands. All of them wore obvious weapons in their belts.

"I come in peace," he said, the universal words to use when faced with a dozen armed and possibly hostile aliens. He repeated the phrase in Vandolian, then—felling a bit silly—said it in Carmalite, which made him sound like a monkey as he chittered, grunted, and whistled. But he didn't have a translator handy, and the odds were high they didn't understand any of these languages.

One of them held out a weapon and pointed it at Chip. He ducked and rolled, grabbing his own burner, and while on the ground, shot at the alien, killing it.

Another alien had already had another weapon pointed at him, and again he tried dodging. The next-to-last thing he remembered was the sting as the beam shot out, hitting his right leg, and looking down, and seeing no leg there.

The last thing he remembered was a motion behind him, and turning just in time to see another alien conking him on the top of his head with the butt of its sidearm.